MEN UNDER FIRE

THE GRAYCE WALTERS ROMANTIC SUSPENSE SERIES - BOOK 3

JACKI DELECKI

CHAPTER ONE

Sergeant Nick Welby forced himself to look up at the plane roaring above him and ignore his primitive instinct to break into a run. His heart punched against his chest in painful thuds. A Boeing 737—not enemy fire. Seattle's Fremont neighborhood—not Afghanistan.

He took a calming breath and then another. The hipster neighborhood, filled with buzzing cars and rushing crowds, ratcheted his already revved-up nervous system, making every sound and movement chafe against his jangled nerves like an open wound.

Talley, Nick's military partner, a bomb-sniffing canine, strained against her lead.

The golden lab, like him, was tense and hyper-alert, waiting for disaster to strike. Both he and his dog were on sick leave. A month had helped to heal their physical injuries, but neither had made progress in calming their stress reactions. They both saw and felt danger everywhere every day.

He stared up at the refurbished warehouse situated on the waterway to Puget Sound. Adrenaline surged through his body at the idea of walking into the unknown building. He was sweating heavily, as if he were still in the heat of the Registan desert instead of the August summer day in the Northwest.

A white-and-black sign hung on the warehouse: *Grayce Walters, DVM, Animal Acupuncturist.* He bent and petted the attentive dog. Talley's soft chocolate eyes echoed the feelings stuck in his throat. "I don't like it any better than you do, but this doctor will help you."

Nick didn't have a lot of hope for his own recovery, but he couldn't let his partner suffer. Doc Samson, the Welby family's veterinarian, had sworn by the amazing skill of this doctor. He paused and blew the air out of his constricted lungs and then pulled the door open. He'd do anything to help his partner heal from the IED explosion that had almost taken both their lives, even walk into this dangerous unknown.

Nick's mind and body were at ease after the hour with Dr. Walters. Doc Samson was right-on—the tiny woman had special gifts. Having been raised on a horse farm, Nick had immediately recognized the veterinarian's intuitive connection in relating to and comforting animals.

Simply being in Dr. Walters's presence was restorative, as evidenced by Talley sleeping soundly on the floor. As Talley's handler, he was connected to the dog at a level most people couldn't understand. When his partner relaxed, he felt the same.

Dr. Walters, looked up from her note taking. "I'd like to treat Talley once a week for the next three months. You live in Auburn. Will it be a problem to drive into Seattle?"

"Not a problem, ma'am. I'd do anything for this dog."

She leaned across her desk. "Do you swim, sergeant?"

"Yes, ma'am." He didn't get what swimming had to do with acupuncture.

"I'd like you and Talley to start swimming in a lake or deep river. It's important you do it together."

"Lake Youngs is close by our family farm. Talley and I can swim there."

"Water will soothe Talley's ratcheted up nervous system."

Why did he feel as if the doctor wasn't talking just about Talley?

"Don't do any training around the swimming. Talley needs a real break from her work. Her senses, especially her focus and her nose are working overtime. She'll have a break in the water."

He nodded. "It will be great to swim after our morning runs."

"Sounds like we've got a plan. Let's see how the swimming works." Dr. Walters stood from her desk and walked toward the door. "I can hear that my assistant is back. She'll make your appointment for next week."

Talley sat up with the doctor's movements. With her front paws planted forward, the usually hyper dog stretched her spine and then slowly hoisted herself to follow Dr. Walters. He couldn't explain exactly what had happened, but like Talley, he felt a deep sense of relaxation. For the first time since he had arrived stateside, he could breathe calmly and catch glimpses of the contented man before the war. He and a tranquil Talley followed the doctor to the outer office.

Dr. Walters stopped suddenly in the doorway. A young, curvaceous woman was balanced on the stool, reaching into cupboards, as she sang the painful lyrics from Nirvana's song "Sliver."

When she stretched her entire body forward, her short black skirt inched higher, giving him an incredible view of her sweet, rounded backside. He swore under his breath at the tempting sight. She wore fishnet tights and thigh-high boots that were right out of every red-blooded male's fantasy.

His whole body tightened, not in danger but in hunger. Lust and need hummed through him, an invigorating feeling that he hadn't experienced in a very long time.

He and Dr. Walters stood frozen. Dr. Walters didn't want to startle her assistant. Nick didn't budge as he reveled in the almighty view.

As if sensing his stare, the young woman turned and jumped off the stool in one graceful movement despite her high-heeled boots. She turned and faced them with a big smile. She had no idea what fantastic torture he suffered. Her tight World of Warfare T-shirt hugged her amazingly stacked body. Heat and anticipation drummed through his body.

Her dark, slanted eyes and her full lips matched her perfect body. He couldn't believe there could be such a beautiful woman. Dumb-struck by her appeal, he stood and stared.

She stared back as if trapped in their electric connection.

"Hollie, can you make an appointment for Talley and Sgt. Welby?"

Dr. Walters's voice startled him to attention. He had been over-come by his primeval response to the young woman despite Dr. Walters's presence.

Her name was Hollie—a prickly flower, like her piercing above her eyebrow; her red lips vibrant and lush like the berries in the long winter months.

Hollie turned toward Dr. Walters. "How long will you want to see them?"

"I'd like to see Talley once a week for the next twelve weeks." Dr. Walters smiled at him before walking back into her office. "You're in good hands now. I'll see you and Talley next week."

Hollie then bent and petted Talley's head. The golden lab, usually fully on guard, didn't flinch or react to Hollie's touch. In fact, Talley leaned into her hand. It appeared both he and Talley felt the same about Hollie. Nick watched her black-painted nails rub along Talley's head.

"She's a beauty." Hollie's voice was low and caring.

Nick couldn't believe he was about to say aloud, *you're the beauty*. His entire world was spinning sideways—first the acupuncture by Dr. Walters and now this incredible woman.

"What day next week works for you, Sgt. Welby?" Her voice was husky and sexy as hell. He was a goner. How could this woman get any better?

He stepped toward her. His need to get closer was overpowering. "Call me Nick."

Hollie had a flush of pink on her cheeks as if she could read his thoughts, his needs. Her clothes and stance were bold, but there was something vulnerable in her eyes. She fluttered her thick eyelashes, and the moment was gone. "Nick, Dr. Walters has openings next Tuesday afternoon."

He angled his body into a protective but possessive posture— unbelievable for him since he never got near to anyone. You never knew who had a bomb strapped under their clothes. With this woman, he couldn't stop himself from wanting to touch her, to run his hands through her long, dark hair. "Talley and I can come back whenever. We're flexible." Suddenly the words rang true. He might be able to break away from his lonely, rigid schedule to make room for...

He tried to not stare at her chest but at the World of Warfare logo with the mystical fairy creature. He pointed to the character on her T-shirt. "Galachel?" He liked that she hadn't chosen one of the avenging, angry, war-hungry goddesses.

Hollie's perfect skin reddened. She whispered in shock, "You know Galachel?

He looked at her chest again. Oh, man, he shouldn't have done that. "Are you a girl gamer?"

Her striking eyes flashed. "Yeah. What about you?"

"I played a lot when I was deployed. Not much else to do on the off hours."

"Yeah, I played more when I was..." She stopped herself and looked down. "It must have been hard...you know being away..." Her voice got quiet, filled with sympathy.

Did she know about the IED explosion? He didn't want her to think of him as wounded. He didn't like thinking of himself as wounded. "Talley and I should be heading out. But we'll see you next Tuesday."

And like a good soldier he knew it was time to retreat.

CHAPTER TWO

Hollie refolded the T-shirts on her friend's vendor table at Pike Street Market. A group of Scandinavian tourists from the Alaskan cruise ship had totally demolished the carefully organized display. Why a group of white-haired women with canes and walkers wanted to examine and touch the World of Warfare T-shirts, she hadn't a clue.

Their interest in the next stall, showcasing Lonnie's potholders made from retro fabric, was understandable, but the elderly women's interest in mythical creatures from a video war game was incomprehensible. Like their marauding Viking ancestors, they had gone down the entire row of day stalls in Pike Place Market, invading and pillaging.

She straightened the stacks of Galachel, the T-shirt she had been wearing when she'd met Sgt. Welby. She refused to think of him as Nick since that would be crossing a boundary of their client relationship. She had told herself repeatedly he was a client and nothing else when she remembered his blue eyes and the crinkles around the bright orbs from too much sun. She had already spent too much time analyzing her unusual reaction to the hunky soldier.

She smoothed the pile of her favorite Ellie design. *Play like a Girl* in bold red letters splayed across the T-shirt with an avenging war goddess, spear in hand.

Ellie had modeled the goddess's image after Hollie's dark, slanted eyes, black, curling hair, and her tough personality.

Hollie smiled at a male Japanese tourist. The young dude held up a T-shirt with a red dragon flying across a netherworld of purple skies.

"Blood Fire from World of Warfare," Hollie said.

He smiled and pulled out a twenty-dollar bill from his wallet.

Hollie nodded.

Obviously not fluent in English but fluent in video games, the kid bought the T-shirt.

Hollie searched the crowd for Ellie bringing their lunch. She hadn't eaten much of a breakfast and was desperate for a square slice of DeLaurenti's pizza.

She spotted Ellie making her way through the narrow aisle filled with humanity. Ellie held the cardboard box close to her chest. She skillfully weaved in and out of the sea of tourists, a plastic bag filled with their Cokes hanging from her arm. Hollie's mouth salivated at the sight of the pizza box and the anticipation of biting into the thick, chewy crust and the melted cheese.

Opening the box that Ellie had handed her, Hollie took a deep whiff of the garlic tomato sauce and breathed a sigh of blissful nirvana.

"Long line?"

"Yeah, out the door and onto First Avenue."

Hollie took a bite of the pizza. Her taste buds exploded with the heavy garlic. It was even better than she'd expected.

Ellie pulled the two stools together behind the stall. Hollie perched on the edge of the stool and placed the familiar box on her lap. Ellie took a big bite. "How did you do while I was gone?"

Hollie unscrewed the top of the Coke bottle and took a big chug. "Better now. I was starved."

"Thanks for coming down and giving me a break. I really appreciate it."

"I don't know how you can stay so nice and polite. I'd start screaming and raving if I had to deal with all the cruise ship passengers who have no intention to buy but have to touch everything."

Ellie snorted. "No, you wouldn't. You just like saying all those badass things."

Hollie snorted. "I am a badass. Have you forgotten how I took that motherfuck-hole Zane down?"

"It was the first time I saw you in action—the way you *roshamboed* him was fricking awesome. You were the only one willing to stand up to him."

Hollie didn't want to remember Ellie's abusive boyfriend who'd pimped her out to keep his heroin habit going. "It was all about pure rage. I sure had a lot of anger back then."

"After you kicked him in the groin and then sucker-punched him, you looked just like Badb, the Irish war goddess. You know, the goddess with black hair and black eyes who took the form of a crow."

Hollie spoke around the pizza in her mouth. "I'm not sure the image of a crow is a compliment."

"My life changed when I met you." Ellie's voice quivered. "And look at me now."

Ellie looked nothing like the thin, emaciated, homeless waif Hollie had met on the street. Ellie's blondish-brown hair was pulled back in a ponytail; her whimsical T-shirt had a cow with a giant bell and a chubby squirrel, both non-players in World of Warfare. Ellie had embellished their wide eyes with long eyelashes, making them adorable and fanciful.

"I hope that if anyone was messing with you, I wouldn't try to emasculate him, but I'd use my aikido."

Ellie laughed loudly. "Good to know that you've harnessed your killer instincts."

"Kind of..." Hollie didn't want to acknowledge that she hadn't come close to letting go of her deep-seated anger toward her meth-producing father. She wasn't sure she'd ever be able to. And this was all part of the problem with Sgt. Welby. He was big and strong, and she always wanted to decimate powerful men. But something about him didn't arouse that rage. In fact, just the opposite. It was obvious Sgt. Welby carried his own pain. And for the first time, she didn't want to strike out at a dominant male.

Hollie shifted her feet on the stool as she watched a harried mother with two small children trying to negotiate their way through the throng.

Ellie's hazel eyes searched Hollie's face. "You're worried? Something happen at work?"

"No..." Hollie shook her head. "It's all good." She wasn't ready to share her confused feelings with Ellie, who she considered more of a little sister she was responsible for protecting.

"Is everything okay with Dr. Walters?" Ellie took a sip of the Coke.

"Working too much, but nothing new there."

"I can't believe how generous she and her friend James have been to me. I would never have been able to get this business started without their help."

"Yeah, the boss and James are really cool."

"I still can't believe this is really happening. I made seventy-five bucks today. Me making money."

This was Ellie's first month as a vendor, and everyone had told her the summer months were when you made the money. May through September—tourists and cruise ships were the golden pig at Pike Place Market.

CHAPTER THREE

Nick was back in Fremont, making his way across the congested street. Like his first visit, he jumped at every noise and movement—the hassled pedestrians checking their phones, the planes overhead, and the honking cars, barking dogs, and screaming children. He couldn't stop his brain from assimilating and assessing potential threats. Talley strained on the lead. With her spine straight, her nose extended, she absorbed every detail and every smell.

The commotion and noise flicked along Nick's ramped-up nervous system, but a more powerful feeling drove him forward. Spurred on by hope, he was willing to endure the sensory overload. For the first time in years, he was inspired to get close, close to a dark-haired woman with unfathomable eyes that shared his suffering.

Nick and Talley entered Dr. Walters's office building without hesitation, immediately comfortable from their last visit to the old, musty building.

Nick had no excuse for showing up three days before his scheduled appointment. As a man of control and precise tactics, he was shocked by his own behavior. He had driven an hour without an explanation for his and Talley's sudden appearance. He was honest enough to admit that, despite his military honors for bravery in action, he was afraid.

His buddies would give him shit if they could see him now—nervous to hit on a woman. He climbed the stairs to the second floor. He was modest about his appeal, but women had always come easy for him. Over six feet, with boyish looks, he was attractive to women. Hell, he had started being pursued by girls in middle school, and women's interest hadn't diminished. His interest in women, beyond sex and release, had been nonexistent until last week. And he had no idea why. Was it part of seeing Talley relaxed, or was there more to his fantasy about the office assistant?

Talley's nails clicked on the wood floors as they approached the door. Nick's heart beat erratically, his palms were sweaty, and his mouth was dry.

Hollie looked up from her desk as he walked through the door. Surprise registered on her face as she stood and came around her desk. Her hair was piled on top of her head in a high ponytail, and she wore a soft white dress that clung to all her curves. Her sweet and innocent look was a fist to his chest. He was having trouble moving air in and out of his lungs.

"Talley, Sgt. Welby, is something wrong? You don't have an appointment today."

She looked young and virginal, nothing like the dominatrix that his male mind had created in the late nights. The swimming regime recommended by Dr. Walters to help Talley was taking the edge off the long days, but the nights were still bad. And when he woke from the same nightmare, he lay in bed and fantasized about Hollie, her incredible bod in the tight black skirt, fishnet stockings, and black boots, and her gentle touch.

She looked closely at Talley. "Is Talley ill?"

He couldn't speak but stared at the enticing woman as his heart thudded against his chest like a marching band drum. He shook his head. "No, we're good. Really good." God, he sounded like a simpleton. He could feel his ears burning in embarrassment. "We were in Seattle and thought we'd stop by. That's not a problem, is it?" Of all the lame shit to say.

"Oh, I'm glad nothing's wrong." Hollie bent and patted Talley. "It's good to see you, Talley," she crooned in a soft, alluring voice.

Talley's ears perked up, and her body relaxed at Hollie's voice.

As she was bent over Talley, he tracked the creamy angle of her neck and a coiled black curl. He could feel her heat, and he caught a whiff of her flowery fragrance.

She didn't look like the badass woman of just three days ago. She was soft, womanly, and alluring.

When she stood up, there were mere inches between them. He wanted to rub his thumb along her plump lower lip. He wanted to do a hell of a lot more.

She turned her head and caught him staring. Pink color crept up her neckline the same way she had blushed when he'd recognized Galachel on her T-shirt.

She moved back around her desk to put space between them. He didn't want to intimidate her, but he was having trouble dampening his needy reaction to this woman. He wanted to chase her behind the desk. He wanted to leap over the desk and kiss her mindlessly. He needed to get himself in control.

Talley watched Hollie retreat behind her desk and lay down on her stomach, her head resting on her paws as if waiting in antic-ipation.

His partner clued in to any heightened tension from Nick, but at this moment, his dog understood there was no cataclysmic danger except, of course, to Nick's heart.

"Dr. Walters is working, but she'll be glad to know you're here."

He hadn't come to see Dr. Walters. He had come to see Hollie, to reconfirm the incredible connection he had envisioned between them in his long, lonely nights. He had to know he wasn't deranged.

"And Talley can meet our office dog, Mitzi."

Talley's head came up with the mention of her name. "Are you sure? Talley is pretty wound up..."

"I'm sure the dogs will get along. Mitzi's a sweetheart." Hollie moved the papers around her desk. "Do you want something to drink while you wait? It's pretty hot out there today."

"This is paradise compared to the Dashti Margo."

"Dashti Margo?"

"The desert region in southern Afghanistan."

"Wow. I can't imagine what it was like for you to be in a strange place so far away from home." She examined his face as if she saw the exhausting toll his tours had taken upon him.

She shifted in her chair and then cracked her knuckles. "You sure you don't want anything? Water? Mint tea?"

"No, thank you. Talley and I are good." He stepped back from the desk, trying to give her more space. She was acting cornered, as if she was apprehensive of him. He knew he was coming on too strong, but the need to get close to this one woman was relentless.

"Talley looks more relaxed than at the last visit." She raised her arms to redo the ponytail, a nervous gesture that pulled her dress tighter across her chest.

He forced himself to look away from the way the soft material outlined her full breasts.

With the movement, the sleeve of her dress fell back to reveal a spiraling snake that wrapped around her arm.

He had to swallow against the tightness in his throat and the way his body clenched in response to the sexiness of her tat. "We've been swimming like Dr. Walters recommended. It really has helped both of us."

"Oh." Her lips were a pale pink, not the racy deep red from the other day. His need to touch her, kiss her was getting ridiculous. He really needed to get his shit together. This interaction wasn't going at all like he'd thought it would go do down. He'd assumed she was an experienced woman of the world and he'd be able to easily seal the deal. But without her black boots and tight skirt, she seemed younger and more vulnerable today. His protective feelings toward her inhib-ited his over-the-top attraction. "You're not were wearing a World of Warfare T-shirt today. I liked the Galachel T-shirt you were wearing when I met you." Oh, he liked more than the T-shirt.

Her dark eyes brightened and she smiled. "My friend designed it."

"Your friend? I thought it was from the Warfare site." He inched closer to the desk again. "Does he do other designs?" He then stood in place, waiting for her to get comfortable with him moving into her space. He used the same method of approach and retreat with the wild horses bought at auction.

"Ellie's dragons are the best. Do you want to see?" Hollie typed fast. Her fingers were long and slender, her nails pink, not black today. "She just started to sell them at Pike Place Market. She's already doing great."

"I'd like to see her shirts." He grinned. He'd be willing to look at fancy dishes if it helped Hollie relax.

"I set up her web page. It's pretty basic, but we're hoping she can sell the shirts both at the market and online." Her enthusiasm for her friend was genuine and endearing.

"Here's her newest dragon." Hollie put her hands on her screen as if to move it so he could see it. She looked up at him with her wide, dark eyes and tugged on her bottom lip with her teeth. "Do you want to come back here to look?"

He wasn't sure if it was the way she bit her lower lip or the way he heard her invitation, but his entire body clenched in expectation.

"Yeah...sure." He walked slowly around the corner of the desk. Talley didn't stir. He bent over her shoulder, inhaling the scent of Hollie, prickly and sweet.

"Man, she's good." He angled his body closer to the screen. *And man, am I a goner.* As if in middle school, he felt like a voyeur, trying to cop a feel or a look down a hot girl's blouse. "Her shirts are better than the Warfare website and less expensive."

"Well, she's got to be careful about the copyright. She has to create her own creatures so Whiteout's attorneys don't come after her."

"I hadn't thought about it, but that makes sense."

Hollie clicked on the next page. "Here's another of her dragons. I love the purple and orange sky."

He hovered over her. He tried to focus on the website, but he was aware of every warm inch of her, every inhalation next to him. He couldn't stop himself. He rested his hand on her shoulder, a light touch, pretending to need her support to get a closer view of the screen.

He felt her slight flinch, but she didn't move away from his touch. Her heat radiated under his hand.

Hollie turned her head up, and he was ensnared in her frank eyes. "Doesn't it look like a desert sunset?"

He could so easily lean in and kiss her, but the move would be so wrong. She was in no way ready. His throat tightened. His voice was winded. "Do you have a favorite? A favorite shirt?" He shifted his body closer until he heard the door opening behind him. He whipped around and moved in front of Hollie.

Dr. Walters, with a large black poodle, stood at the door.

Hollie jumped out of her seat. Talley sat up and flicked her tail in greeting for the doctor.

"Boss, I didn't want to disturb you. Sgt. Welby and Talley stopped by for a visit. He plays World of Warfare. I was showing him Ellie's site."

Dr. Walters smiled at him. "Great to have you and Talley visit." The doctor spoke to the poodle in a soft voice, and the poodle immediately lay down in the doorway. The doctor approached Talley, who waited with her tail thumping on the floor. Dr. Walters bent to one knee and petted Talley. The golden rolled onto her back inviting more attention from the gentle vet.

"Talley looks very relaxed." Dr. Walters's green eyes twinkled as she inspected him. What was it about this vet? He felt as if she were assessing his well-being as well as Talley's, but instead of her scrutiny making him defensive, he felt at ease.

Dr. Walters's calm acceptance of his visit was a balm to him, exactly like his first visit. In this office, the world made sense for the first time in a long while.

Hollie stood at her desk. "I had a brilliant idea about Maddy's T-shirt..." She stopped mid-sentence and waited.

Dr. Walters nodded toward Hollie. "It's okay. Sgt. Welby might give us a new perspective on our search." Dr. Walters turned toward him. "We're trying to locate two missing Marines."

This wasn't what he'd expected to hear. He'd thought it was going to be some discussion on fashion—"girl talk," as his three sisters called it. He looked at Hollie, who was beaming with enthusiasm, and then Dr. Walters, who smiled encouragingly back at Hollie.

"What's your idea, Hollie?" Dr. Walters asked.

"Remember the T-shirt that Maddy wore in the picture?"

"The Teen Feed T-shirt?"

"No, the one in the photo that Angie's mom gave you. James hated it."

The doc snickered. "Well, James isn't exactly a T-shirt kind of guy."

Hollie snorted. "Maddy had on a customized World of Warfare T-shirt. I could do a Google reverse search and find who designed the shirt."

Nick smiled down at Hollie. "That's brilliant."

Her eyes darkened, and her lips curled tentatively into a little smile. Why did he get the feeling that she hadn't received a lot of compliments in her life?

"If you give me the picture from Angie's mom, I could take it to copy store and blow it up while you're at your lecture." Hollie's voice was light and filled with eagerness.

"Sure, anything that might help us find the missing women," Dr. Walters said.

He tried to act casual, but his heart pounded like a thoroughbred crossing the finish line. "Do you mind if Talley and I walk with you to copy store? She could do with some exercise." He and Talley had done a run and a swim earlier in the morning, but he'd use any excuse to spend time with the sparkly woman.

If he hadn't been watching, he'd have missed the tiny twist of her lips into a smile. "Sure, if you want to."

"I guess you've got it covered." Dr. Walters's eyes darted between them. Hollie might not be willing to admit her attraction to him, but he had no trouble if Dr. Walters understood his intention of pursuing her assistant.

"Boss, you should get going. You never know if I-5 is going to be backed up."

Dr. Walters walked back toward her office. "I'll get my notes and head out. I'll take Mitzi with me." Dr. Walters looked down. Mitzi was now lying next to Talley, the poodle's body pressing against the golden.

"Looks like Talley is comfortable in our office. Come whenever you're in town, Sgt. Welby." Dr. Walters's green eyes twinkled.

CHAPTER FOUR

ollie headed down Thirty-Fourth to the copy place with Sgt. Welby and his dog. Hollie's long strides couldn't match Sgt. Welby's. She almost had to run to keep up. He was quiet and tense as they dodged people on the sidewalk. Talley also appeared to be on duty, her entire body alert with her head held high.

Hollie peeked from underneath her eyelashes to look up at the impressive soldier. The sunlight glistened on his angular face and forehead. He definitely had the whole stud package going for him— tall, broad shoulders, sandy-blond hair, and killer bright eyes. He was unlike any man she had known. Like the heroes in the movies, he had the penetrating blue eyes of Ryan Gosling and the boy-next-door look of Chris Hemsworth. Although not as big as the Marvel comic book hero Thor, Sgt. Welby looked as if he could hammer anyone who got in his way.

He looked down at her right as she was checking him out.

Oh, shit.

His full lips curved into a full-wattage, sexy smile. Did he know what his smile did to women? She guessed that he knew the impact of his boyish face and crinkly blue eyes. He must have women throwing themselves at him all the time.

"A penny for your thoughts?"

Oh, buggers. "I was wondering what the tat is on your wrist. Battles you've fought?"

His lashes shuttered down as his jaw muscles tightened. "They're in honor of men from my unit who died."

Going from bad to worse. "I'm sorry."

"It's fine. Lots of people ask," he answered in an abrupt voice she hadn't heard before. His azure eyes stared back at her, and his lip curled into a quirky smile. "I like your tat."

Man, he was adept at switching things up. She wasn't bad at banter, but with Sgt. Welby, the game felt different, exhilarating. She gave him back her best radioactive smile and asked in a sultry voice, "Which one?" Let his mind spin on that for a while. She had never tried to mess with the Captain America types, but she knew how to deal with the assholes on the street.

He stopped mid-step. A little joy buoyed up inside her. She liked getting a reaction from him. She had spent the entire time when he'd come into the office ignoring his hot, forceful stares and trying to hide her reaction.

He gave out a long whistle between his teeth. Good to know she could get to him. "You know you're playing a dangerous game."

She widened her eyes, feigning total innocence. "I've no idea what you're talking about."

He pulled back, his squared chin tucked in, and looked at her from her sandals up her legs to her chest before looking at her face.

Captured like a deer in the headlights by Nick's intensity, she didn't squirm and, she hoped to God, didn't reveal how nervous he made her with his piercing stare. She felt the heat and the scrutiny as if he were touching her.

He was really good at this seduction game. She might not be good at the game, but she wasn't ignorant of the creepy ways of men. As an adolescent, she had been subjected to the filthy minds of her dad's meth associates. With their leering, lascivious looks, the obscene bastards made an innocent young girl feel dirty. For some reason, Nick's stare didn't disgust her—the opposite, in fact.

"Here we are." Hollie reached to open the door, but Nick was ahead of her. Like a real gentleman, he opened the door for her.

"Hey, Hol, what's up?" Nesto leaned across the long white counter. He flicked his head back to shift his hair, dyed jet-black, out of his eyes. With the summer heat, Nesto had given up his worn-out coat and wore a black Slayer T-shirt.

The chrome stud that pierced his tongue flashed as he continued. "Marilyn Manson is coming to the Showbox. I just scored two tickets for this Friday."

"That's dope," Hollie said. Nesto was seriously into metal. He and Hollie had gone to a couple of shows together. It really wasn't her scene anymore.

"We're on, right?" Nesto shrugged his thin shoulders.

"Unbelievable," Nick said under his breath.

Hollie turned quickly. "Are you into Marilyn too?" She would have pegged Nick as an alternative music kind of guy, but what did she know? He moved to her, using his large, muscular size to hover over her. For some reason, she didn't need to push against his closeness like she did with other men who crowded her.

"He's hitting on you when I'm standing right here." Nick didn't lower his voice.

Hollie shook her head. "He's not hitting on me. He's a friend. And stop mean-mugging him."

Nick muttered under his breath. "Right."

Hollie shook her head. "Thanks for the invite, Nesto. But I can't. I'm having dinner with some friends."

Nesto ran his fingers through his greasy hair. "You're turning down Manson? He should be smoking...but not like our Zombie concert."

Hollie felt Nick tense next to her. The dude really needed to learn how to chill. She poked him in the ribs. "The show was mental. Zombie was definitely a showman. All the fire and lights."

"Nick, meet Nesto." Hollie turned her back to Nesto and gave Nick her best threatening look, warning she'd do damage if he wasn't friendly.

"Dude." Nesto nodded at Nick.

Nick said nothing but gave a brisk nod.

She took out the picture from her purse and placed the photo on the Formica counter. "I need to enlarge the T-shirt on this woman." She pointed to Maddy wearing a World of Warfare T-shirt.

Nesto, his fingers covered in tattoos and silver rings, picked it up and examined the picture closely.

"Can you do it?" she asked.

"Depends on how big you want the enlargement. You'll lose details if we try to make it too big."

"I want to enlarge it enough to do a Google reverse search to see if we can find out who designed it."

"I don't think I should go over three by five. I can play around with it and see if I can get it bigger."

"Great. That should be big enough. When can you have it done?"

The door opened, and both Nick and Talley abruptly turned to the sound. A voluptuous woman, decked out in a tight sundress, with long blond hair and designer sunglasses embossed with gold insignias, entered the store. She pulled down her glasses and peered over them. She did a quick glance at Hollie, then a slow perusal of Nick in his worn blue jeans and white T-shirt accentuating his bulging biceps and tight abs. She licked her coral lips.

Nick smiled back at her. He hadn't given her the full-deal smile but enough that she sashayed up to him and Talley. "What a beautiful dog."

The woman wasn't looking at Talley. She was consuming Nick and his impressive bod.

Hollie wasn't up for flirtatious games by golden women and men who both knew their first-class worth.

"I'm out of here, Nesto. I'll pick up the photo tomorrow. Thanks again for the invite."

She turned to get the hell away from all the bullshit. She wasn't going to stay and see if Nick gave Blondie the same devouring stares.

She pulled the door open. Nick was right behind her. Nick's hand came on top of hers. "Let me get it." His hot breath lightly brushed along her neck. "What's the rush?"

"I've got to get back to work." She made the mistake of looking at him.

His blue eyes, twinkling in amusement, pissed her off. What an asshole!

Her anger entertained him.

She didn't take shit. Not from anyone. Not anymore. She marched down the sidewalk.

He grabbed her arm and turned her toward him. "What's wrong?"

She shook his arm off. If he hadn't dropped his hand, she was ready to flip him.

He must have read her intent. All the amusement in his eyes disappeared, and the tone of his voice was grave. "Hollie, what is it?"

She stopped in the middle of the sidewalk. She had no hesitation about making a scene. "Your whole macho man-on-the-make is lame. Go play your games with someone else."

For a second, a flash of upset shone in his darkened eyes, then he stepped closer so that their toes were almost touching. Talley sat down on the sidewalk.

"You think this is the way I act toward all women?" His voice registered both shock and anger.

"I watched you hit on Blondie from Bellevue."

"I did not."

Someone bumped into Hollie, forcing her against Nick. He grabbed her arms to prevent her from crashing into him.

Hollie was about to whip around and nail the bastard who had bumped her. But instead, Nick gently but securely pulled her closer. "I've never acted this way toward another woman. I swear."

"Right. You've never come on hot and heavy before?"

He ran his hands along her arms. "Of course I've hit on women for sex."

"Geesh, even from you, that's brutal." Hollie pulled away from him and walked away.

"Wait. What's wrong? I'm trying to be honest here."

She rolled her eyes. "I've heard a lot of hook-up lines, but yours really sucks."

He walked next to her, but Hollie focused straight ahead.

"You don't understand. I want—"

"Yeah, I get what you want. And it ain't happening." Hollie kept her fast pace, dodging other pedestrians until she got to Freemont Avenue. She had to wait for the light.

"Hollie, can we please just sit for a minute?" He pointed to the long steps by the waterfront building. "You've got the wrong idea."

"Right."

"Just hear me out. Please."

Nick's face was taut with feeling, and his eyes were muddled with emotion.

She couldn't say no.

"Five minutes, that's all you get."

CHAPTER FIVE

N ick's breath couldn't make it all the way down to his lungs. He had totally screwed up. He didn't have a clue what he could say to make it better since he didn't understand his own behavior. He lusted after Hollie, but there was more to it than hard-driving hunger. It was subtle, something that came from her as a woman—her gentle nature and her wounded soul. Her vibrant spirit was far more potent than her incredibly hot body.

She sat on the cement step next to him. Her long shapely legs stretched out in front of her. She had slipped off her sandals. She wiggled her slender, fluorescent pink toenails. How could her bare feet be such a turn-on?

He angled his body to be able to look at her. By the fire flaming in her dark eyes, he had a lot of misunderstanding to repair. Hell, all he had done was smile at the blond hottie. He was used to women giving him the once-over and responded like any red-blooded male. It meant nothing, but Hollie saw it as proof that he was some sort of creepy, uncontrolled freak who hit on every woman. She didn't believe his sincerity, which pissed him off big-time. He thought she had understood him and his genuine interest in her.

"Please let me make this right. I've never met anyone like you."

Hollie snorted. Not the best sign, but at least she hadn't told him to go screw himself yet. And she was still sitting, listening to him. Maybe his years working with wild horses was part of his drive to get close to this prickly woman. He had always enjoyed the challenge of high-spirited horses. In no way would she be easy. Nothing about her said easy. In fact, the opposite. Not that he could tell her, but he got that, underneath the hard-ass act, she hid a whole lot of hurt and fear.

"I'm attracted to you, and I came off way too heavy-handed. But it seems when I'm near you...I..."

Hollie's exotic eyes studied him. And he felt embarrassed by her open, honest gaze.

"I don't go around hooking up with every woman. All I did was smile at the woman in the store. It wasn't anything."

"Tell that to Blondie. She looked like she wanted to devour you."

"There are always women who want to hook up, but it means nothing."

"Hard for you, is it?" She grunted.

"I wasn't interested. She's not my style."

"Rich, stacked blonds aren't your style?" The outrage in her voice was almost amusing, but he'd get clobbered if she saw him smile. She had been ready to do physical damage to him earlier. He was entertained and challenged. He'd like for her to get physical with him but not to harm him.

"Can you give me another chance? I promise to tone down my reaction to you. I can't say that I won't find it hard..." His heart thumped against his chest. He wasn't sure he could promise he wouldn't lust after her. "Talley and I will be coming to the office, and I don't want to make you uncomfortable. If you want me to back off...I will do whatever you ask. I want us to be friends, at least, if that's all that works for you."

"Okay."

"Okay to what?" He sounded too eager.

"I'm cool with friends."

"I'm cool with that." He didn't plan for only friends, but he could behave until Hollie trusted him.

"I don't buy that a guy like you is out of control with lust for someone like me. But I'm cool if you can keep it friendly when you come into the office."

He didn't want to seem too excited. "Great. I appreciate the second chance."

"Everyone always says I'm forgiving." She laughed but without humor.

"If there is anything I can do to help you and Dr. Walters with the two missing Marines, Talley and I are pretty good at sniffing out dangerous situations." He grinned at her, hoping to rescue this disaster of an afternoon.

"Thanks, but at this point, I'm not sure what any of us can do. I'm hoping to track the T-shirt and to find out if Maddy does online chats or forums on World of Warfare. The T-shirt could be random and not connected."

"It's a good start. I'd be happy to cruise the forums to look for her."

"Sure."

"Can you tell me what is Dr. Walters's connection to the two missing Marines?"

"Angie's mom asked the boss to treat her daughter's cat after Angie went missing. The boss is a real softie. She wants to save everyone."

Hollie confirmed what he had already believed. The doctor definitely had rescued her Goth assistant. He didn't know what Hollie had been saved from, but he planned to find out.

"Angie hasn't been heard from since she went searching for a friend from her PTSD group who had disappeared," Hollie said.

"Both women served and have PTSD?"

"Yeah, really crack to have survived the war, and then go missing in Seattle."

"We'll help. Talley and I have experience. But I don't get why Angie's mom would reach out to Dr. Walters?"

"This bit...this reporter convinced Angie's mom that Dr. Walters could talk with Angie's cat. Emily Chow wanted the boss to do a TV talk show after the boss and Mitzi broke up a drug-smuggling ring."

"The little doctor and the French Poodle broke up a smuggling ring? You're kidding, right?" By the way Hollie's eyes narrowed, she didn't find his disbelief amusing.

"Dr. Walters and Mitzi are tougher than you think."

He hadn't meant to upset Hollie. "I believe you." It was obvious she was very protective of her boss and the poodle. "Go on. Tell me about the reporter."

"Emily Chow is still hoping to make a name for herself on the boss's back. She told Angie's mom that the boss could find her daughter by talking with the cat."

"That is pretty nervy of Emily Chow."

"*Nervy* is not the word I'd use."

"I'm sure you'd be able to find a more descriptive one."

For the first time since they'd sat down, Hollie laughed, then gave him the sweetest, most tentative smile. "I swear a lot. It's a bad habit. I'm trying to clean up my act since, once in a while, something spills out at work."

"I don't think you should change anything about you." Nick wanted to touch her hand that was close.

Hollie stood up. "I've got to get going. I've got a project I'm working on."

Nick tried to hide his disappointment. "Yeah, okay. Talley and I should head out. Thanks again for the second chance."

"No problem." And she walked away, ponytail bouncing and hips swaying. Oh, she knew what she was doing to him, and she was enjoying it.

Nick shouted, "Talley and I'll see you in a couple of days.

She turned around and gave him the same flirty smile she had flashed when he'd asked about her tat.

"I know."

Nick couldn't stop the wide grin across his face. Oh, yeah. Hollie wasn't going to be easy, but he was up for the challenge.

CHAPTER SIX

Hollie stood in front of the towering brick mansion. She had never been in any house this large or this impressive. What did she know of mansions with perfect yards and artistically arranged flower beds with blossoms spilling onto the walkway? She had grown up in a rotting, mildewed shack in the woods outside of Darrington, a lumber town in the foothills of the Cascade Mountains, seventy-five miles northeast of Seattle.

Aunt Aideen must have been watching for her. The dark green door with an impressive shiny knocker swung open as she approached.

"Hollie, you made it." In her bright blue caftan, the silver-haired woman greeted Hollie with arms open wide. Everything about Davis's aunt was big. The woman was almost as tall as her nephew but louder, splashier, and totally in your face. Hollie immediately recognized a kindred spirit. She didn't know Aunt Aideen's story, but obviously Aunt Aideen didn't take crap from anyone, including her nephew, the hunky love interest of Hollie's boss.

"I've got cold lemonade waiting. You must be hot after the bus ride."

She did feel hot—not from the bus ride across town but from replaying her earlier interaction with Nick. She had tried to distance herself from him and the effect his dark, inviting looks had upon her. When she'd stormed out of the store, he'd seemed to understand her difficulty to admit any interest in men or any vulnerability. He had apologized, trying to make her feel more comfortable. No man had ever actually considered her feelings or understood her uneasiness.

Aunt Aideen took Hollie in her bulky arms and gave her a big hug. Although Hollie was above average height at five seven, she felt engulfed and small in the older woman's embrace. No one but Aunt Aideen had ever blatantly ignored Hollie's hands-off attitude. Now Nick, like Aunt Aideen, ignored her cool defiance.

"Come inside where it's cool," Aunt Aideen insisted.

They stepped inside the tiled foyer.

"I wish Mitzi could've come. With Davis in DC, I'm missing my weekly visit. Grayce has promised to bring her over next week."

Aunt Aideen studied her face. "It's more than the heat that has you looking frazzled."

Davis had made light of his aunt's psychic talent, but Hollie assumed he was joking. The last thing Hollie wanted was to dissect the unfamiliar feelings Nick stirred within her with Aunt Aideen. Hollie leaned forward to look inside the house. "This is some palace."

Aunt Aideen's eyes remained focused on her face. Hollie knew she hadn't fooled the perceptive woman. Then she smiled and relaxed, as though sensing that Hollie did not want to discuss it. "Why don't we go into the backyard; there's a wonderful breeze." Aunt Aideen gestured toward the entranceway with her thick hand, adorned with a large moonstone ring. "While we have our drinks, I'll tell you more about the project I want you to tackle."

Hollie tried not to gape as she followed Aunt Aideen through a massive living room with towering windows, well-padded couches, and elegant, colored rugs on the tile floor. The entire house she had grown up in could fit in this living room. She balked at calling their shack a family home. That place was the front where her parents conducted business—selling the meth they cooked in the woods.

She'd never seen so many beautiful objects assembled in one place except at the Seattle Art Museum. But Aunt Aideen's house didn't feel like a display to be kept at a distance, to not enjoy or touch. The home and its amazing collection felt welcoming.

Hollie paused to glance at a picture of Davis as a young boy, holding his mother's hand. She wondered how it would feel to have a mother holding her hand and looking at her with such love. "It's hard to believe Davis actually was small."

"He was always large. Such a tragedy that his mother died so young. He was very close to her." Aunt Aideen plowed forward through a swinging door and disappeared.

Hollie followed close behind into the dining room and then into a major kitchen. She gazed around at the glistening stove and refrigerator, the tiled countertops, the herb-filled pots on the windowsill. "You must love to cook."

Aunt Aideen gave one of her deep belly laughs. "I'm a terrible cook, but I like to entertain. You'll have to ask Davis about my cooking abilities." And the idea made her laugh some more.

Aunt Aideen pointed to a tray on the center island. "You carry the tray outside, and I'll get the door. I decided we'd have high tea without the tea since it's so bloody hot. Have you ever done high tea?"

Hollie shook her head.

"I thought not. This will be fun, and we'll get recharged to tackle our work." Aunt Aideen proceeded to the back door and held it open.

Hollie lifted the hefty tray.

"We can use two trays if it's too heavy."

"It's cool. I got it."

Hollie carried the tray out the door into the backyard. On each side, ten-foot hedges gave a sense of total privacy—a secluded haven with a spectacular western view of Puget Sound from Queen Anne Hill.

"Put the tray here, dear." Aunt Aideen pointed to a glass table with a red umbrella.

"Although high tea is British, and, as Scots, we shouldn't love anything British, we appreciate that it's a splendid and civilized custom. When they were young, the girls, Davis's sisters, and I used to have tea parties. Now, years later, I have tea parties with their children. You'll have to join us when the children come. We have a grand time."

Aunt Aideen sat and waved toward the chair across from her. "Of course, Davis hated high tea. Not enough food for a growing boy, you know. And elegant rituals aren't exactly a boy's idea of entertainment."

Aunt Aideen dished fruit onto a plate adorned with pink and green flowers on its border. She cut a wedge of gooey cheese and added crackers and cookies to the plate. She handed the plate with a white, pressed napkin and silver fork and knife to Hollie. "You may pour the lemonade."

Hollie felt nervous, unsure of her manners. The full extent of her dining out experience had been fast food and Denny's, never in such a hoity-toity fashion with everything so perfect and pristine.

She kept her head down and peered at Aunt Aideen through her eyelashes. Aunt Aideen seemed oblivious to Hollie's trepidation.

Hollie poured the lemonade carefully into each crystal glass.

"Please start." Aunt Aideen served herself. "You must tell me what you think of the cookies."

Hollie took a bite of the tiny cookie. It melted in her mouth, all buttery with a taste of lemon. "You made them?"

Aunt Aideen guffawed. "Of course not. I've never had the patience for baking. How about you? Are you a baker?"

If reheating a frozen pizza counted as baking. "Nope. I've never had the time or interest to learn, but I might someday." She was about to lick the sugar off her fingers and caught herself at the last second.

"Oh, I think you're going to learn to cook—and many other things. I see a great future for you."

Oh, no. She braced herself, hoping to hell this wouldn't get weird with psychic shit. She didn't believe people could look into the future. She didn't believe in fantasies. She didn't really believe in much. When you've spent all your life surviving, you don't have time for otherworld mumbo jumbo.

Aunt Aideen burst out into a loud chortle. "Oh, my goodness. Davis has warned you about me, hasn't he? I can see it in your face."

Oh, shit. Now she was caught. She didn't want to get Davis in trouble, but she couldn't lie to Aunt Aideen.

"You don't have to worry about protecting Davis. I know exactly how his logical brain works. And I couldn't be happier that he's found his match in Grayce. She's the perfect antidote for his skepticism."

Hollie didn't know what to say and wasn't sure she should be privy to her boss's private life. It was more than obvious that Davis was one whipped man when it came to her boss.

"I think you should trust your instincts about the young man who has you befuddled."

Hollie was about to take a sip of lemonade. "What?" She stopped with the glass in mid-air. "There isn't..."

Aunt Aideen raised both eyebrows. How did Aunt Aideen know about Nick? The boss would never share private stuff.

"Uh..."

Aunt Aideen waited expectantly. "You should trust yourself. You've developed great insights into people from your life experiences."

Hollie put the glass down on the table. "He's, like, all-American. Probably the star high school quarterback who dated a cheerleader." She rolled her eyes. "I'm not exactly a candidate for dating regular guys." She felt a wave of disgust and shame. "I've never really been on a date. Do you think I should tell him about living on the street after our first or second date?" She started to crack her knuckles but stopped herself.

"I don't think you're obligated to disclose anything you don't want to tell." Aunt Aideen spoke quietly, but Hollie felt the force of her words. "It's your story and yours to share, when and if the circumstances feel right."

Hollie kept her eyes down and busied herself spreading the oozing cheese on a cracker. She didn't want to see pity or sympathy in Aunt Aideen's eyes.

"You have nothing to be ashamed about. I know very little of your past. The important part that you need to remember is, when I look at you, I see a strong and resilient woman."

What crap! Aunt Aideen living in this fancy house. What did she know?

"Both my parents were meth addicts and drug dealers." Hollie leaned back and cracked her knuckles. "I'm not exactly the girl you take home to meet the parents."

Aunt Aideen didn't flinch with Hollie's attempt to rattle her. She leaned across the table and looked directly at Hollie. Now Hollie was the one to flinch with the older woman's steely gaze. "If I know anything about young men, he isn't interested in your childhood or in your parents. Besides you aren't responsible for how badly your parents behaved." Aunt Aideen's lips lifted into a little smile. "I like him already. He has shown great insight to see beyond your great beauty to detect your big heart."

Hollie fingered the fork. Why did Aunt Aideen think Nick could see her big heart? Embarrassed by Aunt Aideen's praise, she felt heat moving to her face. Unaccustomed to compliments, she was used to deflecting them. She couldn't really respond with her usual response of "Bullshit."

Aunt Aideen patted her lips with the snowy-white napkin. "I'm confident it will all work out. Young love is always turbulent at the beginning."

Was this one of Aunt Aideen's predictions? Did she really believe she and Nick could be together?

Aunt Aideen leaned back in her chair. "Let me tell you about the project and the help I need."

Unsettled by the abrupt shift, Hollie only nodded.

"My foundation has been providing financial assistance to women in developing countries, helping them set up their own businesses. I've a new project supporting Tibetan, Newar, and Nepalese women who weave cashmere shawls. The cashmere is collected by Tibetan nomads near Mount Kailash. I have fabulous pictures from my last trip, and I wanted you to add them to the website. You'll have to sort through hundreds of my pictures and decide how to showcase them on the website. Grayce tells me you're tech savvy."

"I'm okay, but I'm surprised your foundation doesn't have a web designer."

"Yes, Martin is the web designer. But these pictures are very special to me. I wanted a woman's eye to find the right pictures to showcase the strength and hope in these women's faces. I think you're the perfect person for the job."

"But...but."

Aunt Aideen lips curved into a big grin as she lifted the pitcher. "More lemonade?"

The sun beat down on Hollie through the open bus window. The sun wouldn't set for another two hours, but Aunt Aideen had been insistent that Hollie leave the house by eight p.m. She hadn't wanted Hollie riding the bus at night. The unfamiliar and sweet feeling that Aunt Aideen worried for her safety made her thoughts jump to Sgt. Welby. He'd be the kind of man who'd be protective—evident in his care of Talley and reflected in his tat in memory of his men.

She had another fifteen minutes in the scorching-hot bus before arriving at her apartment. Thanks to her job with Dr. Walters, she now could afford her own digs—a room in a dilapidated house in the University District. She wasn't bothered that she didn't live in a mansion and that her house was shabby, the paint was peeling, and she hardly had any hot water. For the first time in her life she had her own private space with a lock on the door.

She had worked at Aunt Aideen's desk for several hours, running through hundreds of pictures from the trip. She had lost track of time, staring at the amazing faces of the Tibetan and Nepalese women, weaving cloth to survive in that impoverished, isolated region.

At first she had suspected that she herself was just another charity case for the older woman, but after being immersed in the pictures, she was glad Aunt Aideen had chosen her. She loved the shape of women's faces—their deep black eyes and their pure joyful smiles. And she realized that neither she nor the women in the photographs were charity cases. Aunt Aideen helped people not because she felt any obligation or duty or in order to make points in high society; she helped people because of love. She couldn't believe her luck that Aunt Aideen had entrusted her with such an awesome job.

She understood why Aunt Aideen wanted the page to be something special, because these women were special. Aunt Aideen believed in her ability to do a good job. She'd work hard not to disappoint Aunt Aideen.

A cool evening breeze wafted through the open bus window. Before meeting Dr. Walters at Teen Feed, she had never had anyone who believed in her. Now she had both the boss and Aunt Aideen. Her heart swelled with an alien emotion—contentment, a feeling she wasn't sure she could trust. But for the first time, her world wasn't chaotic but steady and secure.

CHAPTER SEVEN

Nick took one shuddering deep breath before opening the door to the acupuncture office. Unlike his visit a few days ago that had gone sideways, he had a game plan for today's interaction with the prickly but perfect Ms. Hollie.

Anticipation and hunger licked along his spine as he opened the door. Which persona would she present today—the hot leather chick or an innocent? He'd liked her as both. He simply liked everything about her.

Hollie stood in the doorway of Dr. Walters's office with her back to him, giving him enough time to check out her sweet backside in tight blue jeans before she spun around.

By the way her dark eyes narrowed, he had been caught enjoying the honeyed view. One minute near her and already he had blown his plan of cool and collected approach. He tracked up her tight black T-shirt with an avenging war goddess that looked a lot like the woman in front of him with her ebony hair and fiery eyes. Instead of her hair down around her shoulders like the image on her T-shirt, Hollie's black, shiny hair was twisted on top of her head and held in place with chopsticks. He would like to see her let down her hair, but mostly to see the heavy curls splayed across his pillow.

She had ditched the ephemeral goddess T-shirt for the angry, aggressive one. Was her T-shirt a message to him to be wary of women on warpaths? Somehow he thought it might be, and the thought pleased him. Did she have any idea that presenting herself as a dare just revved him up? And he was every bit the man to take on the challenge.

She had her feet apart and her dark eyes staring directly at him. Oh, she was a tempting provocation. "Talley and Sgt. Welby, right on time for your appointment today." She gestured for them to proceed directly into Dr. Walters's office. "Dr. Walters is ready to see you."

He wasn't going to get to chat her up before the appointment. Not in the least intimidated by her bold posture, he moved closer, gently crowding her against the doorjamb. "You'll be here when Talley and I are done?"

He liked the way her eyes widened and she raised her defiant chin. "Of course. I work here. Where did you think I'd go?"

He leaned down close to her ear. "Thought you might try to hide from me."

Her spine stiffened as she stood taller. She tilted her head, show-casing her exotic eyes and her strong-boned cheeks. "I don't run from anyone."

He couldn't help his need to inch closer and feel her heat, and her chest puffed up in umbrage. "Good to know."

He smiled at her exasperated, loud exhalation.

Nick entered the doc's office with Talley wagging her tail. He wasn't exactly keeping to his plan of cool and helpful, but Hollie's baiting look of *wait till I get you alone* had his whole body thrumming with tension and excitement.

Dr. Walters hadn't moved from the chair behind her desk. He

knew she had watched him hit on Hollie. And although he didn't want to look like some oversexed jerk, he couldn't stop smiling when he greeted the vet.

The petite woman stood and walked around her desk. She bent to pet Talley, to rub along the big dog's chest. "I can see that you are both feeling well today."

Talley sat alert as the vet petted her, then she lay down on her side in total trust. They both were doing a lot better. And Dr. Walters gave him the perfect segue. He needed Dr. Walters's approval of his pursuit of Hollie, and his need to be of service. He'd never disrespect a woman and never insult a woman like Dr. Walters. Knowing what he and Talley had suffered, he was committed to help the missing Marines with PTSD.

"Ma'am, may I speak to you before we get started with the appointment?"

Her lips parted into a small smile. "Please." She pointed to the chair in front of her desk.

He waited for her to sit before he did.

"Is this about your extra visit?"

Nick sat up taller. Oh, shit. Was she going to warn him off? He hoped not, since he didn't think he could stay away.

"Yes, ma'am. I'd feel more comfortable knowing you don't mind me...coming to the office and... I'd like to help with the search for the missing Marines. It would give me something else to focus on—"

"Beside your interest in Hollie?" He hadn't noticed how Dr. Walters's green eyes could change colors. They were lighter, almost mischievous.

"I mean no disrespect to you, ma'am, or to Hollie."

"Of course not. I think you could be a great help with your military experiences and your tech savvy. And I know Hollie would appreciate your help."

"She would?" He couldn't hide his interest. He also knew he couldn't fool Dr. Walters. She definitely was perceptive and something else he couldn't nail.

Dr. Walters laughed, a light laugh like a garden wind chime. "I'm pretty sure she would."

He leaned forward, closer to the desk. He was dying to ask if Hollie had said something. "That's great news. Thank you, ma'am. Talley and I won't let you down."

"Hollie is a very smart and talented woman. She's had a lot of challenges in her life. I'm assuming you won't pressure her. Not that Hollie would allow it."

"Of course not." Nick would never break his promise to Dr. Walters, and he'd struggle, if needed, to temper his intense attraction to her office assistant. He could man up to the tantalizing trial.

CHAPTER EIGHT

"Hide from him! Of all the bullshit!" Hollie muttered under breath as she stomped back to her desk. Despite the heat wave, she wished she had worn her high-heeled boots so she could make a loud statement.

Nick Welby knew exactly how much he had rattled her, and he also knew she couldn't go ballistic since the boss was sitting right there. Hollie had been forced to stifle all the threats of harming his body parts.

And hadn't he enjoyed her misery? His slow, quirky smile said he'd gleaned every tormented, twisted word she'd had to swallow.

Wait until he came out, away from the boss. She'd a few choice things to say or maybe not. He was expecting her to be all fury. Hollie laughed out loud. Oh, she was going to enjoy making him squirm with her own dark, lustful looks. Two could play this game.

In the meantime, she had been able to check out the T-shirt designer's website now that she'd traced a Google match for the T-shirt. His website was called Earthbro. What a loser since the guy was all about violence.

She really hoped she could find a connection to Angie and

Maddy. The boss had said nothing, but Hollie knew she felt pressured not having any leads for Angie's mom.

Hollie was startled when the boss's door opened. She had become engrossed in the hilarious chatter of the stoned gamer dudes and had lost track of time.

Nick and Talley came out alone. Perfect. No barriers to her aggravating the shredded dude with the boss in her office.

Nick's face had softened; his eyes were now clear as if he'd had an acupuncture treatment too. She didn't know how Dr. Walters did it, but clearly the boss healed both the owners and the animals.

Nick put on the whole macho guy thing, but Hollie had recognized at their first meeting that he was suffering from the effects of the war. He was hypervigilant and tense. From her months on the street, she recognized his situational awareness, the compulsion to ensure the environment was safe. In her life, she had only worried about her own safety—much simpler than Nick's and Talley's burden of protecting others.

At this moment, she lost her need to make him squirm. He looked relaxed. She was glad that Dr. Walters had given him relief from the pain.

She jumped up from her chair. "Looks like Dr. Walters's treatment helped."

Nick jolted in surprise.

His reaction made her smile. Had he thought she would attack him? Since she had considered leveling him, she was amused.

The tightness in his jaw and neck were gone. "Yeah, I don't know how she does it, but the acupuncture really helps Talley relax."

Interesting that he didn't mention that it helped him. Yeah, macho thing. After her time with the guys on the street, she understood male posturing.

"I spoke with Dr. Walters about helping with the search for Angie and Maddy."

"You did?"

"I wanted to get her clearance in helping you with the chat

rooms. I didn't want to overstep my place." He closed the space between them.

There he was doing it again. Didn't seem like he minded overstepping with her. And for some damn reason, she actually liked him getting close, which made no sense since she usually hated anyone invading her space. She never liked being cornered.

"I told her that it all depended on you and whether you wanted my help, since you obviously know what you're doing."

Her heart whacked against her T-shirt. Right when she wanted to protest his involvement and hold on to her control, he acted sweet and considerate by respecting her choice. How could she say no? Finding the women was the focus. And she could use help to look through the forums. It'd be lame to turn down his help.

She turned and sat behind her desk. "Sure, whatever."

Talley lay on the floor as Nick followed her. He propped his hip on her desk, making himself comfortable. "I've got my laptop in my car. I thought Talley and I could go over to the coffee shop —Insteads?"

"You mean Milsteads?"

"Yeah, the one across the street. I could start to cruise the chat rooms unless you got something from the Google search."

"I found the website designer. I went through all his T-shirt designs, and he's really into cataclysmic shit. But his website is called is Earthbro."

Nick shook his head. "What a douchebag name."

Hollie grinned. "Exactly my thought."

He gave her the irresistible, full-wattage smile—emphasizing his perfect white teeth and the crinkles around his eyes.

Hollie's heart pounded. Her throat constricted. Did he have any idea how much she... liked him?

"Why don't Talley and I head over to Milsteads and see what we can find."

"Sure."

"Can you meet up after work and we could compare sites?"

Her heart pulsated in her throat, and her stomach fluttered. She rearranged the pencils on her desk, then started on the paper clips when she caught herself.

She could feel his penetrating scrutiny. He definitely knew he had threatened her in the most basic male-female way.

"Sure, my place isn't air conditioned. I'd love to be in a cool place."

With his hot gaze locked on her, he clearly wasn't buying her lame excuse for working with him. "Great. We'll head over and get to work." He pulled on Talley's lead. "Come on, girl." He stopped at the door. "You'll show, right? You're not agreeing just to get rid of me."

She paused and tapped her finger on her chin, taking time to consider her answer. "Payback is hell, isn't it?"

He studied her intensely as if he were touching her. He closed the door, but she could hear his deep chuckle as he strode down the hall.

CHAPTER NINE

Nick parked himself and Talley at the corner table in the coffee shop, opting for private and cozy—perfect for socializing with the cantankerous Ms. Hollie. He checked his watch again—after five. He wondered if the argumentative assistant planned to ditch him. He had never been stood up by a woman before.

He didn't like the idea that Hollie had perceived his charm with the ladies and was messing with him. His body drummed with anticipation tweaked by her sassy retort that payback was hell. He wanted payback—in the very basic male manner.

He glanced up at the front door for the hundredth time. Reading horny, stoned dudes' chatter had been entertaining for the first half hour, but he was ready to spar with a real woman. Her lateness was torment.

He thought of all the carnal ways he'd like to pay her back, make her lose the anxious look she worked hard to hide. He wanted to have her relaxed, enjoying herself. Not a great idea in a public place to get a boner. Must be all the damned sex-starved-guy talk on the forums.

Hell, who was he kidding? Hollie had him ready just with her smile. He definitely lusted after her, but she drew him in; something hopeful, deeply buried in him, responded to her. He couldn't believe how her face had shone with kindness and compassion when he'd come out of Dr. Walters's office. He loved the soft, tender woman beneath her hard edge.

Her badass act was a shield. He understood being defensive. He had been shielding himself from the moment he'd returned home to the arms of his concerned family. The wretched way his mom and his sisters couldn't hide their worries... He had even caught his dad checking him out, struggling with the idea that his son might have changed irreparably, become a stranger. Nick had manned up and given them what they wanted to hear. He was doing fine. He and Talley were both healing. His reassurances calmed them enough that they'd backed off, as he had intended.

He looked up when the door opened. Hollie had arrived. Her face was flushed from the heat. One wisp of hair was plastered across her forehead. She toted a black shoulder bag decorated with a picture of a kitten. When she spotted him, her lips curved into a tentative smile.

He and Talley both stood up and watched as she made her way across the crowded room. One big guy with a bushy beard and fat stomach eyeballed her. Looking around the room, he realized all the dudes, who hadn't looked up the entire time he had been here, were following Hollie's movement. She was a sexy woman in her tight blue jeans, tight T-shirt.

Possessiveness surged through him. He wanted all the nerds to get their heads back down to their screens. She was his, all his. The bearded dude said something to her, probably some dumb-ass pickup line. Hollie shook her head and laughed. He wished he'd chosen the table by the door so the guys couldn't watch her sashay across the coffee shop.

Behind the counter, the barista who had earlier had been hassled stopped working and propped his arms on the counter. "Hey, Hol. You're looking hot today!"

Hollie's lips bent in a very friendly and familiar way. She stopped and chatted with the tattooed barista. The guy kept copping looks at Hollie's chest, probably bullshiting that he was interested in her T-shirt.

Nick stood up. He was a man on a mission. He commanded Talley to wait and went to Hollie's rescue from the oversexed dude. He covered the space between him and Hollie in a few strides. As if sensing him approaching, she turned, shifted her weight onto one hip as if she were about to tap her foot, and then she rolled her eyes.

What the hell? Why was she censuring him?

The intimidated barista scampered back to his espresso machine. Nick took a slow, easy breath. Suddenly very confused by his aggressive response, his hair-trigger reaction—exactly what the counselor had described. He looked around the room. All eyes were on him. He needed to get his shit together.

He wasn't the jealous or the possessive type with women. Part of the reason he'd been chosen to work with Talley was his easygoing manner. He and Talley were known for their chill attitude.

Embarrassed and unsure, he turned to go back to the table and wait for her.

Hollie, as if she perceived his scrambled emotions, stepped toward him and touched his arm. "You're looking a bit wired. Did you drink too much espresso waiting for me?" She had never touched him before, and he felt her soft touch down his entire body.

Confused by the way her dark eyes searched his face in concern, he could only nod. "Yeah, maybe."

"I want you to meet Eric. He's a crazy gamer." She widened her eyes and nodded her head toward the gamer, signaling him to make nice with the guy. "I told him about how you and I are both into Warfare."

She leaned on the counter. "Hey, Eric. Come meet Nick."

Eric, with a diamond stud in each earlobe, wiped his hands on the cloth hanging out of his waistband and walked over. He eyed Nick warily, then offered a handshake.

Nick shook his hand. "Heard you're quite the gamer."

Hollie nudged him with her elbow. "Eric has made it to dungeons level."

Nick nodded and smiled, but he still felt unsettled. Maybe he wasn't ready to be out in public. His hot and heavy pursuit of Hollie was a way for him not to deal with his issues. He found himself sinking down, wondering what the hell was he doing here, playing hero for missing Marines when, at some level, he was MIA himself.

He wasn't aware that he had missed the entire conversation between Hollie and Eric until Hollie linked her arm into his. "Talley's waiting for us." She led him back into the corner.

Her closeness and gentle touch eased the tight pressure in his chest and his pounding heart.

He looked down at her glistening face, and his anxiety faded. "I wasn't sure if you're were going to dis me."

"Had you guessing, did I?" she teased with the sassy voice he liked.

His laugh was a bit rusty. "You know you did."

"We got an emergency call, and I waited for Dr. Walters to finish."

Talley's tail started to thump when Hollie got closer. "Talley, aren't you a hip dog, hangin' in Fremont." Her high-pitched voice made his dog's tail thump louder.

Hollie dropped his arm, and he felt the sudden loss of her touch. She went down on one knee and hugged Talley. The dog licked her face before flipping to her side to offer her stomach.

The afternoon sunlight pouring through the window shone on her ebony, twisted hair, reflecting almost-blue highlights. She rubbed Talley as she talked in a quiet, soothing way. He was glad to see his devoted dog getting the kind of attention she needed. He and his dog were starved for human touch, connection.

His therapist had explained his withdrawal from his family and friends as survivor's guilt. He and Talley were the only ones who hadn't died in the explosion they had been responsible for preventing. Somehow, when he was near Hollie, he forgot for a few moments.

"Guess it's showing that Talley and I've needed a woman's touch."

She twisted to look up at him. Her dark eyes shuttered.

Shit. He had done it again. Shit. Shit. Shit. He didn't intend the comment to be sexual. But how would she know the difference between sincere feelings and male primitive?

He bent over to help her up. "Did you order a drink? Can I get something for you?"

Ignoring his outstretched hand, she stood and swung her big tote bag onto the floor.

"Nah, I have a water bottle." She was detached as she sat down across from him and pulled out her laptop. "Have you found anything?"

Talley shifted so that her head lay on top of Hollie's sandals.

"I've been following three forums, looking for any kind of talk about violence since you told me Earthbro was into that kind of stuff. So far, it's mostly adolescent guys letting off steam." He avoided saying anything about randy guys making all types of sexual jokes.

"Yeah, but I'm not sure they're only teenage boys. There are grown men on the site acting no different than horny teenagers."

"You know all guys' minds are wired that way—no matter what age."

"Whatever." She rolled those dark eyes, and the shiny piercing on her eyebrow bobbed. He didn't like the idea that she had violated her beautiful skin with a piercing and the large tattoo.

Her head was bent as she logged in to her computer. He stared at the way her long, thick eyelashes fanned on her cheekbones. "I can't really come up with an easy way of finding Earthbro. He probably has many character names."

"Exactly. It's why I've been looking for someone who was spouting off about blowing stuff up. But that's, like, most of the players," he said.

Hollie laughed, a deep, husky laugh that rushed down his spine and his lower body.

He shifted in the chair, avoiding eye contact—afraid she'd see how she affected him.

He cleared his dry throat. "Have you thought about just emailing Earthbro and asking about Maddy's order?"

"I did think about it, but why would he give that info out? I was hoping we could discover where he hung out and follow the chatter as a lead to Maddy. Angie's mom said that Maddy had family problems and had lived on the streets. Also, the boss thought she might have a past with drugs. Street people use chat rooms to do drug deals and all kinds of crazy shit."

He wanted to ask her how she knew about the street, but he could imagine Hollie's defenses growing into an unscalable brick wall if he asked about her past.

"Your idea is that we try to watch the chatter for possible patterns other than the randy or stoned guys?"

He enjoyed sitting here with her, working together. She was sincere and had committed herself to finding two total strangers. He had to wonder how much these women's issues touched her own struggles.

"I was surprised. Dr. Walters doesn't seem like the kind of person who'd want you to call her *boss*."

Hollie's dark eyes lightened. "She prefers Grayce, but it doesn't feel right. I'm her assistant, and her clients respect her." Her voice had gotten warm. Whatever was in her past, Hollie was attached and very loyal to Dr. Walters. He admired loyalty.

He wanted to tell her that she was an amazing woman, but instead, he took a sip of his decaf. Hollie wasn't the kind of woman to smother with compliments.

Hollie's cell rang. She fumbled in her kitty tote bag searching for the ringing phone.

"Hey, boss, what's up?" Hollie stood up and walked outside. She held up her hand to signal she needed a minute.

Talley went into alert mode. She tracked Hollie's movement out the door. With her eyes focused on the door, the big dog stood at attention.

Nick rubbed the bulky head. "It's okay, girl. She's coming back."

He would've laughed at Talley's anxious posture if he hadn't seen the parallels between them.

He and Talley both fixated on the door, waiting for Hollie. He had no idea if evening calls were part of her routine.

Within a few minutes, Hollie came back into the shop. He immediately noticed the change in her posture. Her neck and shoulders were pulled back and tight, and she chewed on her bottom lip. Something had happened, and she was worrying.

He stood and pulled her chair out. Distracted, she sat and absentmindedly caressed Talley's head.

"This is insane. Angie just showed up at the office."

"Angie? Like, the missing Marine Angie?"

She sat back in her chair and massaged her neck, realizing how much she had tightened. "She doesn't know where she's been the last weeks. She had some sort of head injury that her MD thinks triggered a flashback."

Icy fear hit Nick straight in the back of the neck. He avoided the tragic stories of other soldiers with PTSD. He hoped he hadn't given any sign of the dread gripping him.

Hollie searched his face and then leaned toward him. "Hey, I'm sorry. Didn't mean to be harsh."

"Don't worry about it."

Hollie rolled her eyes. She wasn't buying his abrupt manner.

He didn't want to show any reaction to his deep-seated fears or the disappointment that their work together might be finished. "Did Dr. Walters say anything about Maddy?"

"That's the whack part. Angie asked the boss to help find Maddy."

She leaned back in her chair and crossed her legs. He tried to look away from her long legs as he imagined peeling her out of the jeans. "Why would a Marine ask Dr. Walters? What about contacting the police?"

"Angie wants to protect Maddy's privacy—not wanting her drug use to become a legal problem. And of course, the boss, the bleeding heart that she is, has agreed to help."

He could hear the affection and respect in Hollie's voice.

"What are they going to do?"

"The boss doesn't know yet. Angie's going to call her tomorrow."

"Talley and I could help."

Talley's ears perked up at the mention of her name.

Hollie shifted in her chair. "I'll tell her that you offered. The boss asked if we could keep looking for Maddy in the chat rooms."

"No problem." He couldn't believe in less than two weeks since meeting Hollie, he and Talley were sitting in a crowded coffee shop and not waiting for disaster to strike. Earlier, he had been close to having a meltdown, but Hollie's calm touch had brought him back. Who'd have known that a pierced, tattooed woman with attitude would bring him and Talley back to the world of the living?

CHAPTER TEN

Hollie dropped onto her desk and covered her head with her arms, struggling to suppress the scary thoughts of the boss's car accident. Anxiety clawed through her; she couldn't shake the fear. Last night, the boss's brakes had failed, and she had rammed into a tree.

Hollie kept the panic at bay. She had to put on a professional front with all their clients. The boss was depending on her. She was determined not to fail. In her most authoritative voice, she reassured each client that the boss was recovering, while she was the one who most needed the reassurance. The boss was her family—her only family.

The boss's outrageous best friend had been serious and brief when he'd woken her this morning to give her the upsetting news. Without his usual flamboyance, James had given a solemn description of the boss's concussion, leaving her worried that he was trying to spare her the scary details. Cold terror slithered up her spine and into her neck. What wasn't James telling her?

She was scanning the calendar, checking each day's appointments, when the office door opened. Nick and Talley had arrived. In her distress, she had completely overlooked their plan to work together.

Nick came straight to her. "What's wrong?"

She shook her head, trying to avoid looking into his concerned face. She was determined to keep it together, not to get all emotional.

He gently grasped her by the elbow and pulled her up into his arms. And this time, she let him. He wrapped her in his heat.

"It's going to be okay." His large hands soothed her, gliding up and down her back.

She stood still, unable to move. No one had held her with such tenderness. No words would come out of her mouth.

Talley leaned into the side of her leg, as if also trying to offer comfort.

He bent over, his face close to hers. His intense focus warmed her. "Did something happen with Maddy?"

She swallowed hard past the aching knot in her throat. "The boss..." The words came out forced and breathless.

He searched her face. "Something happened to Dr. Walters?"

Hollie had kept it together until Nick arrived. Now she couldn't stop the rush of tears that dripped down her cheeks. "She was in a car accident last night." The words filled the silence with stark emotion.

She felt his body clench against her as he squeezed her tighter.

"She has a concussion, but James reassured me that she will be okay. Nothing to worry about."

Pressed against his hot body, she didn't want him to let her go. "Is she in the hospital?"

His quiet self-control steadied her. "She came home early this morning."

He tucked a curl behind her ear. "She must be okay if they sent her home, right?"

She wasn't sure if it was because of his composed voice or his quiet strength, but her panic eased. She could almost breathe normally.

"I'll take you over to see her if you'd like. I'm sure seeing her in person will help."

The empty black void of terror was receding. She reminded herself that she was safe, and her boss was safe. Nothing terrible was going to happen to her. Her whole body shuddered in relief.

He tightened his arms around her. "You okay, honey?"

She tried to make herself push away but instead stood still, reveling in his unwavering composure, his slow, measured breathing against her chest. She inhaled his masculine scent of pine and musk. She needed to pull it together, but being held by Nick Welby changed the entire messed-up, whack day. The tender, safe embrace of Nick Welby could become an addictive habit.

Hollie pushed out of Nick's arms when she heard the office door open. Ewan Davis, the boss's jacked boyfriend, strode into the office. He looked like hell. His blue oxford shirt, his gray slacks, and thick, black hair were rumpled. His eyes were dull and bloodshot.

Talley, who had been sleeping in front of the desk, sat up. Hollie rushed past Nick to get to Davis. "Is something wrong? Is she worse?"

Davis was tense, his muscles clenched under his wrinkled clothing. "She is fine. And is going to stay fine, if I've anything to say about it."

Hollie stared at the agitated male, all pumped up with angry adrenaline. He looked primed for a fight, not overcome with worry.

Davis inspected Nick as if he might take him on.

Hollie stepped in front of Nick to protect him from Davis and his seething, black mood.

Nick chuckled and pulled Hollie to his side. "You don't have to protect me, but it's very sweet.

"I'm Nick Welby." Nick offered his right hand while keeping Hollie pinned against him.

"You're the military guy, right?" Davis inspected Nick's shredded body and then shook his hand. "You'll do fine."

"Davis, what is going on? You're crazy intense even for you...

You're being all—" Hollie shut her mouth abruptly when Davis's dark brows flattened.

"Someone tampered with Grayce's brakes. Her car accident was no accident."

A combustible mix of fear and rage shot through her. She pulled away from Nick. "What the f?" She reverted to her unnerving habit of cracking her knuckles. "Who would want to hurt Dr. Walters? She is the gentlest woman on the planet."

Davis had again gone all dark and brooding. He paced in the tiny anteroom. His angry, tense strides raised the emotional chaos firing through her.

"I'm not sure yet, but I've got to believe this had something to do with the missing women. She's gotten too close."

Nick pulled Hollie against him. "I can help."

Davis turned and inspected Nick again. "Grayce has told me that you're spending a lot of time in the office..." Davis stopped whatever he was about to say and looked at her. "Working with Hollie on the Internet angle, right? And since you're here, can you keep an eye on Grayce when I can't be here? She'll also have Mitzi with her."

Hollie bristled at being overlooked. Didn't she count in Davis's plan? Hollie wasn't about to be left out. She had grown up taking on men who preyed on innocents who were weaker. "I can guard the boss. Remember my aikido."

Davis's lips curved into a half smile. The little hairs on her neck prickled at his amusement. She pushed away from Nick's side. "Listen, Davis, I can handle myself in a fight."

"I'm sure you can." Davis shrugged his shoulders. "You can help Nick."

"Help Nick!" Fury raced through her body. She might have to take down Davis, although he was one big sucker.

"You and Nick work it out. I've got to get back to Grayce."

Hollie didn't like the slippery way Davis handled her involvement. But, hell, what did he know of her abilities or street fighting? He was raised in a fancy-schmantzy house like his aunt's.

Talley, as if understanding all the drama was over, laid on her side and went back to sleep.

Davis headed toward the door. "Hollie's got all my numbers. I'll be in touch." He paused with his hand on the doorknob. "Watch your back. I don't like the feeling I'm getting about this perp."

CHAPTER ELEVEN

Nick was pissed. He tried to give Davis a break, but not when it came to dissing Hollie. Davis was wired because his woman had been threatened. Nick would be as unreasonable if anyone had injured Hollie. He needed to rein in those terminator feelings. Right now, he had to deal with one red-hot, worried woman whose feelings had been hurt.

He understood how Hollie rolled. With her feet parted, her cute chin thrust forward, she was ready to kick ass. Her fighting-mad stance wasn't fooling him, although she was doing a darn good job of hiding her hurt and fear. She was battle ready, and he was the only man left standing.

"Hollie."

She spun around as if ready to lash out. "What?"

If she could focus her fire on him...sexually. Maybe they'd get to that later—a man could hope. He refrained from smiling, knowing she might decide to grind him into mincemeat.

"You know I'll do whatever it takes to keep Dr. Walters safe." It'd be foolhardy to add, "And I plan to keep you safe too," since he could possibly get hurt. Obviously Hollie didn't buy the idea of a man's protection. He guessed that was because she had never had the protection and love of a man worthy of her.

"You're upset," he said calmly.

"Really? You guess? I'm supposed to let some macho men protect her?"

He inched his way closer to her. He couldn't touch her yet. "You can't take that stuff about Davis seriously. He was all revved up, doing his caveman shit because the woman he loves was threatened."

Hollie cracked her knuckles. "He doesn't even know you, but he looked at all your ripped muscles and thought you'd be better than I was in taking care of the boss."

He inched a little closer. He was approaching touching range. "Honey, that's a guy thing—men sizing each other up."

She snorted. And he wanted to kiss her. How crazy was that? "Dr. Walters must have told him about my training."

Obviously stressed from this morning's news of the car accident, she hadn't taken the usual time with her appearance. Her hair was in a crooked ponytail, she had applied no makeup, her lips were pale, and she had on a white girly T-shirt with a cow and squirrel. How cute was that? She looked young and sweet, and all he wanted to do was take her in his arms and hold her, take away all her hurt.

He shrugged his shoulders, trying to appear nonchalant. "I was going to be here to work with you on the chat rooms, so no big deal, right?"

Her almond-shaped eyes got flinty. "Sure, whatever." She started to walk around him to get to the desk.

He grasped her arms. He felt her smooth, soft skin underneath her T-shirt. "Talk to me. I want us to work as a team. We've been doing great working on the chat rooms, haven't we?" He couldn't resist running his hands up her arms. And she didn't bolt away. "We can guard Dr. Walters together."

Her lashes lifted, treating him to the sight of her confused dark eyes. "How?" Her voice was breathless, and it took all his self-control not to kiss her. That would start fireworks, but not the ones he was hoping for.

"You tell me. You know Dr. Walters's schedule. You can coordinate when you or Davis aren't going to be available, and I can fill in."

Her pinched eyebrows and her puckered lips said she wasn't believing it. He wanted to run his thumb along her disgruntled forehead and full, pouty lips.

With Hollie this close, her scent filling his head, he spoke with more ease than he was feeling. "You do agree our focus has to be on the chat rooms to find Maddy since it's the way to keep Dr. Walters safe."

"But who would want to harm the boss?" Her voice was low and pleading, like a small child trying to understand the unfair workings of the world. "She heals animals."

He pulled her closer and tucked the errant curl that had fallen out of her ponytail. "I don't know, but you and I are going to do our best to find them. Okay?"

She looked up at him, her dark eyes velvety with emotion. "Okay."

He soothed the pulse on her pale throat with his knuckles.

Her pink lips parted in a shallow breath, and immediately he was lost.

"Honey, don't hurt me."

She looked up at him stunned. And he bent to kiss her. He touched his lips against hers, allowing her to pull away. She had startled when he'd first touched her, but now she stood still, waiting, not exactly reciprocating but not trying to emasculate him.

He pulled her tight against him. And pressed harder against her softness to open up to him. She was still. Frozen. Not kissing him back, as if she didn't know what to do, but not withdrawing. She kept her lips on his and let him explore her lips with his tongue. Realizing Hollie might not be the experienced woman he had assumed, he pulled himself back from immersing his tongue into her hot, wet mouth.

Instead, he kissed her gently, savoring her sweet taste, making promises with his mouth to cherish her. With her soft breasts crushed against him, he could feel every small breath and gasp. She'd had a rough day, and he wouldn't take advantage of her vulnerability. She was all about control. He'd never hurt or embarrass her.

He pulled back from her lips and placed little kisses on her closed eyes, then along her jaw, and finally on her pert nose.

"We're a good team, aren't we?" He rubbed his thumb against her swollen lips and smoothed her lopsided ponytail.

Hollie's eyes had softened; her warrior posture had faded.

She looked so unsure of herself. It swelled his heart with tenderness. But Hollie wouldn't like any softness to show.

"Is there anything else you need to do here?"

She looked so befuddled that he couldn't resist giving her one last gentle kiss on her warm lips.

She leaned against him, and it took all his control not to kiss her the way he had fantasized—his tongue thrusting in and out, imitating his deepest desires. Instead, he rubbed her back, resisting the urge to grab her tight tush and press her against his erection.

He lessened his hold on her and continued to run his hands back and forth, then he stroked her ponytail. Soothing her, he'd definitely gotten her mind off Davis, although he tortured himself in the process.

"Honey, why don't we go to Milsteads? I bet you skipped breakfast."

He waited, then pushed her chin up with his fist. "Did you eat breakfast?"

She shook her head. The color on her face and neck receded as she gained control of herself.

He watched her recover and waited for the tongue-lashing, but she surprised him.

"I am hungry. I was in a total rush this morning to get to the office."

He didn't plan to give up the ground he had gained in penetrating her defenses, in allowing him in her space. He brushed her arms. "Why don't you get your laptop? We'll work at Milsteads after we've eaten.

CHAPTER TWELVE

Hollie had settled into her usual table in Milsteads Coffee Shop. Everything was familiar—same randy dudes, Eric working as barista. Familiar, but nothing was the same. Had she been transported to an alien world? Had she time-travelled into someone else's life?

Nick's muscular thigh was pressed against hers. She could feel his warmth through her blue jeans, smell his scent of pine and musk.

She pretended to be engaged in the drivel of the morons on the website, but her heart, head, and world were spinning. From underneath her eyelashes, she kept gazing at his strong profile, trying to comprehend how her resistance to all men had been magically melted away by Nick Welby.

She peeked at the way his snowy-white T-shirt hugged his broad chest and his sky-blue eyes darted back and forth on the screen. He was bent over his computer, and his thick fingers moved rapidly over the keyboard, but every so often, he would lean over and rub her neck or playfully pull on her ponytail.

Hollie Thomas playing cozy with a stud muffin—none of her

friends would believe it. Why would they? She didn't. And she didn't
believe how much she liked Nick touching her.

"Have you seen this player Pony Poo Poo?"

Lost in her reveries, she startled when Nick leaned into her and
turned his computer to show her an avatar of a unicorn shooting rain-
bows out of its butt.

"My sisters wouldn't like their childhood pals being mocked.
They were really into their Little Ponies. Did you play with Little
Ponies? Comb their tails? It was kind of crazy that my sisters, who
had real horses to groom and comb, still enjoyed the dolls."

"I never got into the ponies. I played outside a lot." She didn't
mention she'd done it to avoid her parents' customers.

"You must have been such a cute little girl." He stared at her face.
"I'm trying to imagine you in pigtails."

There was a time when her mother would braid her hair with
ribbons, but that was before the meth. Hollie didn't want to think or
talk about her childhood. "It might be time to hack into the forums
and identify Earthbro by his user ID."

That got Nick off her whack childhood. His posture got all tight
and stiff, and he shifted his leg away from hers. Although she missed
the heat and pressure, she refused to edge closer to him.

He turned and faced her. "You have those skills?"

"Yeah." She shrugged. "Don't you?"

He shook his head. "No. I'm a proficient gamer but not a hacker."

Of course, he wouldn't do anything dishonorable like hacking.
He was a soldier. He believed in law and order and respect for the
flag.

He lowered his voice. "You're amazing."

She was more than taken aback. She had assumed he'd be ready
to report her to the FBI. Not that she had ever done anything that
criminal.

The way he smiled at her, his eyes light with admiration, sent
sensations of ice and heat over every inch of her skin. He leaned
closer, about to kiss her. Without a will to resist, she inched closer.

"My, my. What do we have here?"

Hollie startled at the sound of James's voice. "Oh, my God. James!" She jumped up out of the chair and into his arms. He grabbed her by the shoulders and held her tightly. He whispered into her ear, "How are you holding up, runt?"

James, the boss's best friend, and she had become very close over the past year. He was outrageous and, like Hollie, hid all of his more sensitive feelings behind sarcasm and cynicism. But unlike Hollie, James was sophisticated and definitely dramatic. Without either subtlety or sophistication, she was hard grit and filled with a heap of anger.

She now savored the comfort of her friend. Snuggling closer, she whispered back, "Is she really okay? You're not lying to me, are you?"

"Lie to you? When you'd come after me and kick my ass..."

Hollie snorted.

He pulled on her ponytail. "Remember, we're working on your social graces. No snorting or cracking your knuckles."

"What the f—"

"And no four-letter words. Grayce is fine. A headache, that's it. And she needs to rest."

Not realizing how enormous the strain of the day had been until she had James's reassurances, she let out a big sigh. She turned in James's arms to look for Nick.

"We're being rude." James released her and put his arm around her shoulder, anchoring him next to her side as he studied every inch of Nick's hard, sculpted body.

"And you...must be Nick. Hollie, darling, you've been holding out on me. Why didn't you tell me that Nick—."

Hollie stomped on James's foot before he could say something outrageously sexual and blatantly offensive.

Nick's face was strained, his eyebrows had drawn into an angry line, and his jaw was clenched tight. Oh, shit. Talley was standing at attention next to Nick, obviously responding to Nick's high-alert death threat. How could she communicate that James was gay and more like a brother than a love interest?

She pulled away from James's side and touched Nick's arm. "Nick, this is James. I've told you about him. He's the boss's best friend, remember?"

James ran his hand through his dark, perfectly coiffed hair. "You and Grayce sure like the serious, brooding types. He's not going to injure me, is he?"

Nick shifted his weight and, without any humor, said, "He's thinking about it."

Hollie now rolled her eyes and patted Nick on his chest. "Nick wouldn't hurt anyone. He's a gentle guy."

James laughed. "Darlin', I think you just insulted Nick. I'm not the possessive type, but I've a feeling Nick might be."

When Nick stepped closer, she looked into his bright eyes, trying to decipher his mood. His muscles were clamped in tension. "James, you have to meet Nick's dog, Talley."

James bent and petted Talley's head as the large dog thumped her tail in appreciation. "You're a gorgeous girl." James stood and offered his hand to Nick. "By the way, I'm James Weston. And you're obviously Nick Welby. Grayce has spoken very highly of you."

Nick shook James's hand. "Dr. Walters has been very helpful to Talley."

Hollie wanted James to like Nick although she wasn't sure why. But in James's presence, he was all quiet and remote.

And James was more subdued because he must be exhausted after staying with the boss all night. He did look beat. "Can I get you something? Do you want a coffee?"

"No, thanks. I'm going to go home and crash. I've been in the ER with Grayce."

Hollie shook her head. "Davis came to the office and told us about the brakes."

James flung his hand in his dramatic fashion. "I had to get away from Grayce's house. Davis was in his protective, take-no-prisoners mood. The sparks flying between them were rather painful and entertaining to watch."

Nick loomed over her and raised an eyebrow to remind her that he had told her the same thing. Hollie smiled in acknowledgment.

James was moving his lips silently with "Oh, my God." The heat flamed onto her cheeks with James's fascination with the interplay between her and Nick.

Nick turned toward James as if he knew he had missed something.

James, with his usual cool-dude attitude, spoke as if he hadn't been silently high-fiving her. "Davis is going to keep Grayce safe, but until this is resolved, everyone has to be on their guard. How Grayce gets herself into these situations is still beyond me."

Hollie felt the tension creeping back into her body with the reality of the threat against the boss. "I'm going to guard the boss. Davis asked Nick to watch her when she's in the office. You're going to help too, right?"

"Yes, if she'll let me. She hasn't agreed to Davis's plan. But I think Davis will win on this round. Whoever messed with her brakes meant to hurt her."

Hollie's whole body shuddered in fear with James's blatant declaration.

Nick wrapped his arm around her. "It's going to be all right."

James winked at her when Nick's head was bent over. Thank God for small favors that James had restrained himself from his incendiary comments.

"Listen, runt. You need to be more careful too," James said. "We don't know why or who is after Grayce, so we have to assume it's either her helping the Marines or one of her patients. Which means you also could be a threat to the lunatic."

"I can handle myself."

James nodded toward Nick. "Wrong thing to say, with Nick and Talley ready to protect you."

Hollie pulled away from Nick. "Why is everyone acting like I'm helpless? I know how to take care of myself. I've been doing it my entire life."

James gently chucked her under the chin. "And you've done a great job. But maybe it's time to let other people help."

She didn't like the way Davis, Nick, and now James were all acting protective toward her, treating her like a victim. She had resolved that she'd never be a victim again. Never. "I don't need protection."

James yawned, his perfect white teeth showing as his mouth gaped open. "Too much drama for one day. I'm out of here."

Hollie now felt like an obnoxious child in the middle of a temper tantrum. James started to walk away. She grabbed his arm. "Thanks for coming, especially when you've had no sleep."

"No problem, runt." James hugged her, then looked at Nick. "You're going to have your hands full with this one."

Nick gave his stomach-fluttering, knee-shaking smile. "I'm looking forward to it."

CHAPTER THIRTEEN

After James's departure, Hollie, with her sagging shoulders and her lopsided pony, suddenly looked deflated.

Nick put his hand on her elbow and turned her toward him. "Let's get an early dinner. We've been at this for hours." If he had said, "You look beat," she would've fought him to stay and work.

He ran his hands along her soft, silky arms. "I'm hungry. Aren't you? It's been hours since we ate." He was hungry for this complicated, feisty woman and knew what would help them both get rid of the tension, but in no way was Hollie ready, especially now that Dr. Walters had been injured.

"You sure eat a lot," Hollie said.

"Really? I guess with swimming and running, I need to keep refueling. Should we go to the burger place? You eat meat, don't you?"

Hollie rolled her eyes. "Beggars can't be choosey. I eat anything and everything." She abruptly stopped and shifted her attention to packing up her laptop.

He sucked in a breath, unable to speak. Had she gone hungry? When? As a child? A simmering fury filled his body. The idea of her not having enough to eat overwhelmed him. He felt helpless in the face of her obvious suffering. His childhood had been filled with an overabundance of everything, loving parents and family.

He was going to make sure she never suffered again.

In one vicious gesture, she swung her bag over her shoulder and stuck out her chin. He was getting quite adept at reading her moods. When feeling vulnerable, she always took on her *don't mess with me* attitude.

Risking her wrath, he took the bag from her shoulder. "Let me carry the bag."

Her dark eyes narrowed, and the pierced eyebrow slashed down. He might get pummeled.

"You take Talley's lead. It's good for her to walk with different people so she knows she's not working," he said in a confident voice, acting as if he might get his way.

She opened her mouth, then immediately closed it, her dark eyes expressive of the conflict. She wanted to fight him, but she wanted to help Talley more. He repressed the smile tugging at his lips. He was learning how to negotiate the prickly Ms. Hollie.

Ignoring him, she cooed at Talley. "You ready to get out of here?"

Talley's ears went up, and she stood, ready to follow Hollie.

He stuffed his laptop into her bag and placed it on his shoulder, then handed Talley's lead to her.

"Tell me about James. He's an interesting guy."

He stepped back for her to exit first out of the coffee shop. He tracked her crooked ponytail, bobbing as she walked. He'd never expected to feel an incredible emotional and physical connection for a woman or such a responsibility.

Hollie and Talley walked toward the corner of the busy intersection. Hollie said over her shoulder, "James is the sweetest, funniest guy, and I don't know why you had to go all Tarzan on him."

He tugged on her ponytail. "Honey, I'm always going to react when you're in the arms of another man."

She jerked around so quickly that she pulled on Talley's lead. Talley immediately sat down. "Oh, sorry, girl."

"James was right, you know. I'm crazy possessive when it comes to you." Her face went pale and her eyes fluttered in emotion. He moved closer to pull her into his arms.

She backed away. "Why?" She shook her head. "You don't even know me. We only met a few weeks ago."

"I know it's crazy. It feels a lot longer." He wasn't going to let her distance herself. "And I do know you." He brushed his knuckles along her smooth, honeyed cheek. "I know that you're sensitive to others feelings. You're protective of anyone weaker than you. You're loyal; you're strong. And you're hot with a killer bod."

She parted her lips in surprise. He rubbed his thumb along her full lower lip. He was ready to kiss her as she leaned into his touch.

She shuddered, then shook herself off like a wet dog. "I can't do this." The way her body tightened and her eyes darted back and forth, he thought she might break into a run.

He reached for her, but she lunged away, acting like a cornered animal. "Tell me what's wrong."

"I can't do this." Her voice quivered in emotion. "It's, like, normal. And I'm not normal."

He wanted so badly to touch her but kept his hands at his side.

"You were the quarterback, weren't you?"

"Quarterback?"

"In high school, you were the quarterback, right?"

Hell. What was this about? "What does that have to do with anything?"

Her face was mottled, and her silly ponytail had lost most of its moorings with her violent head movement.

They were having another moment in the middle of the sidewalk in Fremont. He gently gripped her arm. "Can we talk about this privately? Walk Talley along the water?"

She pushed his hand away. "Tell me, dammit. You were the star quarterback?"

He nodded his head. "Yes, I was the quarterback."

"And you dated a bouncy, blond cheerleader, right?"

"Yes. I dated a cheerleader. Why does that matter?" He searched her face, knowing that she was building walls between them, reacting against the intense and scary bond between them. She had to get over her fear. It frightened the shit out of him too, and he had gone to battle in Afghanistan. He couldn't imagine what it was doing to her, but he wasn't going to run or let her push him away.

"Because while you were living the Brady Bunch life, I was..." She shook her head and pushed the long hair tumbling across her face. "I was... Never mind." She marched away, crossing the street, unaware that she had Talley's lead.

He followed her silently. She had a whole lot of pain and anger, and he wasn't sure how to help her.

She walked toward the waterfront path, then stopped and patted Talley. He could hear her low voice as she soothed Talley. Although upset and distressed, she stopped to comfort his dog. She was a loving, gentle woman—the right woman for him.

He let her walk ahead, keeping his distance.

When they had gone the two blocks to the waterfront path, she stopped, turned, and waited.

He didn't try to get close or touch her as they waited at the light. "What did you mean when you said you aren't normal?"

He had a pretty good guess of why she was upset, but he wasn't sure if she would confess anything about her background.

She ignored the changed light and huddled next to a brick building on the corner. "Because while you were having a happy life with your happy and loving family, I was hiding from my father, who planned to sell me to one of his meth suppliers."

He felt sucker-punched—an iron fist hammering him in the head and gut. A killing rage filled his body as his breath came in aggressive surges. Unprepared for the shocking admission, he had no words for the outrage and obscenity of her father.

"I've never told anyone that part of my past." Her lower lip quivered, but she looked directly at him, waiting for him to judge her.

"But you're a really good guy, and now you know why this won't work." She pointed back and forth between them.

He was trying to stay on track, but his mind was clouded with devastating emotions and anger. He couldn't imagine the depth of betrayal by the person who should protect and care for you. He wanted to decimate the man who called himself her father. He shook his head and tried to get a grip. No wonder she didn't trust men and held to her staunch claim that she didn't need anyone.

Her voice was low, overwrought with emotions. If she thought telling him that her father was an immoral bastard would change his feelings about her, she was dead wrong.

With her pitiful voice, her makeup smudged from her tears, and her hair tangled, she was making a mess of setting any distance between them. He was in deep because learning of her terrible childhood only strengthened his resolve to make up for everything she had missed. He was never going to let his tough survivor flee.

"Didn't you have other relatives to take you in?" He chose not to ask about her mother, assuming she was part of the monstrous crime against an innocent child.

"My grandmother tried to protect me, but she didn't have any legal rights."

He tried to imagine her as a young girl coping with the fear and betrayal with no one to protect her. He had to touch her, comfort her, and he didn't care if she tried to nut him. He pulled her tight against him. "I'm so sorry, honey. I wish I had been there for you."

He loosened the remaining hair from the rubber band and smoothed her thick hair down her back. His dog nudged her nose against Hollie's leg. "Even in high school, I was big, and I would've kicked the shit out of your dad before I had him arrested."

She tried to laugh, but it came out in a sob. She buried her face against his chest. He could feel her tears soaking through his shirt.

"I'm sorry you were alone and that there was no one to protect you." He rubbed her back, trying to calm both of them.

She cried quietly, which made it all the worse, as if she were afraid to cry. The only sound was a hiccup as she tried to smother the distressing sounds against his chest.

He tucked the hair covering her eye behind her ear. He kissed the tears on her cheeks, her nose, and her lips.

"Honey, you're not alone anymore. Talley and I will never let anything happen to you. You're safe."

She pushed against his chest with both her hands. "You're not listening to me. I can't do this."

He took both her hands into his. "What, exactly, is this?" She tried to pull her hands free. He tightened his hold. "What have you decided you can't do?"

"Date and shit. You think you need to protect me? I'm fine taking care of myself."

"I know you can take care of yourself. You obviously had no one to take care of you, until now."

"Look at me and look at you. Goth girl with Captain America." She pulled away again, and he let her hands go.

"What I see is a strong, beautiful woman who, despite a shitty family, is loving and gentle."

That gave her pause. Her exotic eyes widened, and she bit her lower lip. "What bullshit. You need to find yourself another cheerleader type. Blond and perfect."

Admitting her shame was difficult, and he'd do anything to help her move past it.

"I'm thinking you're really focused on the cheerleader as an excuse. Are you worried that I'll be like Angie—have a flashback on the street?" He didn't mean to sound aggressive, but she had a way of pissing him off and frightening him at the same time. He was afraid that her deep pain would make her reject him.

"No, I didn't mean... I know you're recovering, but I'm not worried about you that way." Her voice was tremulous and unsure.

Seeing her concern for him softened his reaction. "You're not worried that I might go off."

"Never. It's never entered my mind. You're solid and reliable."

He wanted to kiss her, but they needed to clarify their feelings. He wasn't going to let her hide behind her defenses.

"Okay, so what's this bullshit about me wanting a perfect woman? I'm not perfect, so why would I need a perfect woman? Unless you think I'm shallow. Is that it?"

"No..."

"I want you and only you. Why can't you believe it? That your father was a sick shit has nothing to do with us."

She pushed her hair away from her face. "You're a hero. And now that you know how repulsive my family is, you'll want to rescue me." She wiped her nose with the back of her hand. "The last thing I want is to be pitied."

He loomed over her. "Pity you? I've never woken up every night thinking about a woman I pity. A woman who makes me laugh, challenges me, and has brought me out of my funk. A woman I want under me."

He would have laughed out loud at the shock on her face if he hadn't just declared his feelings for her. He was almost as shocked as she was.

Her mouth was open wide, and her hands were clenched at her sides. "Oh," she said.

He picked up a strand of her silky hair and twirled it around his finger. "'Oh' is all you have to say?"

He could feel her hot breath from her open lips and her shallow pants. "Don't you want me a little?"

Hollie gazed into his eyes. Her black eyes were glassy from the unshed tears. She looked down and nodded slightly.

He lifted her chin with his thumb. "Is that a yes? Honey, help me out here. I'm a desperate man. I don't go around declaring myself every day."

"But Nick..." Her pink lips were parted and so ready to be kissed.

"What, honey?"

"I've never done any of this." She said this in a quiet, unsure voice so unlike her.

"'This' meaning dating?"

She laughed nervously. "That too. I've never dated, but I meant never been with a guy."

Nick got another sucker punch—this time a wallop to his throat and his heart. His brain was scrambled from this newest revelation. Hollie was a virgin? A mess of emotions blasted through him. He had been worried that she had been raped by those sick fucks. He was relieved that she hadn't been traumatized. But sexually inexperienced—a surge of protectiveness and tenderness rushed through him.

"Yeah, is that right?" He brushed against her pale throat and quivering pulse with his fingertips. He wanted to trace the vibrating pulse with his tongue, tasting her.

When she looked up at him, her color was wan, her lips pale, and voice quiet. "My experience with men hasn't been exactly ideal, and I've never met anyone...I..."

"I get it. It'd be pretty hard with scumbags." He shook his head. He didn't need to remind her of the creeps she had to deal with. "I'm glad, honey, that you were never forced."

He brushed his fingers across her cheeks. "You know I'd never make you to do anything, right? Can you trust me?"

She chewed on her lower full lip as she wiped at her tear-streaked face. "I do."

He was having trouble keeping his shit together. He wanted to show her how good it could be to be with a man, a loving man. He wanted to take her home with him to keep her safe in a perfect world.

"I've got an idea."

She pulled her chin back away from his touch.

"What idea?"

"Let's start dating."

"Now you're making fun of me." She started to turn to walk away.

He grabbed her arms and pulled her back against him. He got a whiff of her shampoo and the scent of Hollie. He whispered close to her ear, "You've got to stop running from me 'cause it just makes me want to chase you." He lifted her hair to one side to get better access to her pale, slender neck. He rained soft kisses, nuzzling her neck. "I wasn't joking. Movies, dinners, baseball games. I'll go to artsy stuff if you want, but please, no opera."

She giggled. A girlish sound that was light and joyful.

"And I'm going to spend a great time and effort teaching you how to kiss." He didn't add the other ways he planned to educate her on the mating dance.

In a little, quiet voice, she answered, "Okay."

His body had tightened in readiness. Every muscle was clenched as heat spread through him. What else could he ask for?

CHAPTER FOURTEEN

Brandon Billow huddled next to Maddy on his sleeping bag. She smiled at him, and her shiny blue eyes gleamed. They were in the jungle on the west side of Beacon Hill above the freeway—a greenbelt of trees that the homeless and people on the run with nowhere else to go, had claimed as their own. Their group of eco-activists, really a group of misfits and losers, hid among the homeless to prevent being tracked. Three days before the big bang. He had started calling his mission *the big bang* because it was going to be the beginning of a new and better world in which nature had equal rights with human beings, but he had to be careful not to slip.

"Brandon, what do you think?" The tight, clipped, and miffed voice came from their leader, Jason, the dude with the golden, fleecy hair, and it rattled him back to the present.

Hell, he hadn't been listening to Jason's endless drone of *look how smart I am; look how handsome I am with my blond hair, blue eyes, and seductive smile*. Maddy wasn't here for the cause; she was here to sleep with Jason—as were half the women in their group. And didn't Jason know it.

Always alert to his flock, did Jason recognize Brandon's distraction? Their leader was getting increasingly suspicious. Or was Brandon only getting paranoid as the big day approached? Jason's light eyes examined his face, searching. It was important that he not let Jason see his anxiety. Did anyone else notice his nervousness? He needed to keep his shit together.

Jason was no fool.

"Sorry, Jason. I spaced out."

Maddy poked him. "Hey, this is important."

Too bad Maddy had been attracted only to Jason, or he might have spared her.

He smiled at Maddy. "Sorry, Mad. You're right."

"Okay, D-day is almost here. Let's review everyone's job. Fred, you're in charge of buying the balloons. Remember, they've got to be heavy latex," Jason said.

"Like my condoms, heavy latex for a heavy workout." Fred, who had terrible acne and greasy hair, was probably still a virgin. At least there was one guy in the group who was getting

less than him. Maddy and Teresa laughed, but Erika, a hard-core feminist, rolled her eyes in disgust.

"I'll get the vegetable oil," Jason said in his usual commander-in-chief voice. He reminded Brandon of his CO in military school—always in charge, always the alpha male, and

always beating the shit out of less-than-perfect cadets. Military school was just like home, the almighty male forcing his will on the powerless.

"I still think it's going to be tricky getting the balloons into the meeting." Erika continued to fight Jason's position as the leader. Obviously, she wasn't sleeping with him. "Only four of us are carrying the balloons in our backpacks."

"Are you having trouble with my plan?" Jason challenged.

Shit, he really wasn't up for rehashing the whole discussion of who was willing to be arrested for the cause. He had a record from his

DUI and his shoplifting. He used his criminal past as an excuse for not wanting an arrest now. Maddy didn't want to be arrested because of her juvie record. He and Maddy were assigned to protest in front of Pier 69 to provide a distraction

when the others entered the building. What great irony. He wished he could laugh out loud right now and tell them he had a distraction for them.

"What's so funny, Brandon?" Jason had his eagle eye focused on him. Sweat pooled on his back and under his arms. The urge to break into a sprint seized him. He inhaled slowly, trying to move his frozen lungs. "I was just visualizing the look on the asshole commissioners' faces when you hit them with the oil."

"That's exactly my point." Erika stood. "I want to make sure the timing is right. Brandon and Maddy have to walk in with the pictures of the animals drenched in oil from the spill in the Gulf of Mexico when we belt them with the balloons filled with oil from the audience." Erika continued to give Jason shit about his plan. Same old bullshit as in all his previous groups. Always boiled down to power and sex.

"Brandon and I'll disrupt whatever they're saying when we walk into the meeting and chant 'No spills in our waters,'" Maddy said.

"And when the audience turns back toward Maddy and Brandon, we'll stand and throw," Erika said.

"Tom and Susan are going to this Tuesday's meeting to check out the space," Jason added.

Tom and Susan were the only non-misfits of the group. From wealthy East Coast families, they'd gone to college together and gotten radicalized in environmental issues at liberal Evergreen College. With North Face jackets and expensive haircuts, they both looked and acted as if they could just as likely be working in corporate America as hatching illegal eco-terrorist plots. Except for Maddy, the entire group had been at Evergreen with Jason.

How Maddy had met Jason remained a mystery.

"Wherever we sit, we've got to nail the president and three commissioners," Jason said.

Teresa stood and addressed the group in a grave voice. "I'll be in the front row, ready to record the entire proceedings, the surprise attack, and the arrest, then immediately post on the

Internet. We want the pictures of the oil-soaked commissioners to be front page on national news."

"Any questions?" Jason looked at each person.

Was Jason suspicious? Jason seemed to be watching. Hell, he was getting paranoid. Only three more days.

"Everyone stay low. And only communicate on the World of Warfare forum. We'll meet in two days under the Aurora Bridge."

Why Jason thought a tourist spot was a good meeting place was beyond him. Every tourist visiting Seattle wanted to see the colossal Troll statue under the Aurora Bridge. He reminded himself that it was only three more days of Jason and his whack ideas.

CHAPTER FIFTEEN

Hollie, sitting at her desk, kept her head down and surfed another gamer chat room. She needed all of her self-control to not be distracted by Nick...again. Stationed by the door, with Talley at his feet, he remained on duty guarding the boss for the day. With his new responsibilities, Nick hadn't changed his casual, sexy look of a tight black T-shirt and worn jeans. He looked like a cross between a surfer dude and Captain America.

Since the accident last week, the routine had been the same. Davis brought the boss to the office. Depending on his work demands, Davis would stay until she left for the evening. When Davis had to work, Nick was "on duty." Today Davis had to attend an all-day meeting on security issues in the region. It was a big deal and he couldn't miss.

Hollie checked Earthbro's posting about the newest patch for the Warfare game. The forums were going bonkers about the newest patch that allowed players to meet more characters and play at a more challenging level. Lately Earthbro wasn't talking about blowing things up in the game but more about delivering justice. He seemed to be ramping things up.

Davis was still in the boss's office. He'd be late if he didn't leave soon.

Hollie wondered if the delay was due to Davis kissing the boss the way Nick had kissed her last night. His tongue thrusting into her mouth, as if he would devour her.

Nick must have felt her stare. He looked up and his eyes heated. Her entire insides melted with his intense, possessive look. Who knew that, with the right man, one sizzling look could make you feel heady and irrational?

Her face started to heat. No way did she want to look like an inexperienced woman, daydreaming about his kisses. She had her pride, and she hated to think about him kissing his cheerleader or any other women the demanding way he had kissed her.

She needed to focus. She wasn't going to be mesmerized by one scorching, sexy look by Nick Welby. It was time to hack Earthbro's account and find his IP address to track his postings. They had been surfing the damn gamer sites all week with no interesting chatter.

She forgot about Nick and his tantalizing look as she delved into the guild forum. Hollie was shocked at how easily she had hacked the Warfare website. She had thought they'd have several hard-core firewalls. She had Earthbro's IP address. Hacking into the site and firewall was child's play. A piece of red velvet cake for a gray hat like her.

She startled when she heard Davis's emphatic order from the boss's office. "No, you're not going alone. I won't allow it."

Wow. Davis had definitely been in a mood since the brake incident, but this was insane.

Talley stood up and looked toward the door. Nick raised his eyebrows. "Sounds like a rebellion."

"It must be about today's visit to Mrs. Leary's," Hollie said.

Nick stood up and stretched. And Hollie tried not to look at the way the T-shirt hugged his tight abs and his biceps flexed. She had never liked muscular men until Nick. Who knew that bulging muscles were such a turn-on? But it wasn't Nick's fantastic bod that had her heart throbbing and stomach fluttering. It was his kindness to

Talley and the clients who came into the office, the tender way he touched her, and most of all, the way he'd compassionately listened to the painful details of her desperate family background.

Nick walked over and levered his hip on the corner of her desk. "Davis already filled me in about Dr. Walters's appointment. She goes to Laurelhurst to treat an older woman's cat."

"Mrs. Leary's a dear. She has trouble getting around, so Dr. Walters goes to her house."

Hollie tried not to listen to the voices in the next room, but she could hear the boss's low and insistent voice, then Davis erupted, "Unbelievable. Grayce, you're driving me insane."

Hollie felt prickles of anxiety skirting along her skin set off by the hostility. "No way should he be shouting at the boss. He needs to bring it down a notch. She is very capable of taking care of herself. She's trained in aikido."

Nick shrugged his massive shoulders. "I feel for the guy. There is no way in hell he wants her forced to defend herself."

Hollie jumped out of the chair. "You're siding with Davis yelling at the boss?" She moved around the desk and loomed over him. "You don't believe women can protect themselves, do you?"

He didn't seem able to stop staring at her Kidrobot shirt. She had worn the tight tank and the long skirt that clung to her shapely, long legs to torment him. She was enjoying her ability to rile the composed and collected Nick Welby. "I'm not saying it's right to yell, but I understand where Davis is coming from. He's worried about all the ways things can go wrong. Personally, I know women can take care of themselves, because I have a stunning example right in front of me. And honey, you're killing me in that top."

His appreciative words and hungry look immediately helped calm her. They were all on edge with the worry about the unknown menace threatening the boss's safety.

Embarrassed by her emotional outburst, she said, "He might be worried, but he doesn't need to yell."

"Come here." He pulled her to stand between his legs. "You were too far away." He rubbed her arms up and down. "I'm sorry. I know the shouting upsets you."

She didn't know how he did it, but the simplest touch and she felt all squishy inside. She liked watching the way his bright eyes darkened and his voice got smoky when he touched her.

"You know Davis would never hurt her. It's obvious he's totally a goner." He caught her hand and pressed her palm hard to his mouth and then his jaw, greedily savoring the contact.

Shivers of cold chased along her skin with the touch of his hot mouth.

"He's trying to protect her. He's playing and replaying all the possible ways the nut job might try to get to her. It takes a toll on a man." Nick was good at multitasking. He turned her hand over and kissed a path up her arm to her elbow. Who knew how sensitive the inner arm was?

"Is that what it was like in Afghanistan?"

He paused. She felt the subtle way his breathing changed, his body tensed.

He kept his head down, preventing her from seeing his eyes and his face. "Over there, you were always trying to stay ahead, anticipate...but there are times when you can't avoid..."

"Is that what happened with the men—the stars on your wrist?"

"Where are all these questions coming from?" To her disappointment, his husky, hungry tone was gone.

She pressed closer and ran her fingers along his bristly golden jaw. "I'm interested in you. I'm not trying to be nosy. You don't have to tell me anything you don't want to."

He slowly exhaled and picked up her other hand. "Thanks."

Hollie waited. She told herself that she wouldn't be angry if he didn't share. Secrets took time to share. But she had unburdened herself and didn't want to be the only one exposed.

He held her hand and looked into her eyes. She tried to hide her hurt and shame, but by the perceptive way he examined her face, he read how she felt.

He laced his fingers through hers and released a long sigh. "Talley and I were doing a sweep of the market in Kabul with a small reconnaissance patrol following. That day, it wasn't crowded but was difficult to secure because of the alleys and twisting side streets. Talley kept sniffing in front of a fruit stall, but she didn't sit signaling that she had found a bomb. I yelled to the men to wait, and during the split second, a woman hidden in a side alley ran toward the patrol with an IED underneath her abaya. All the soldiers and three civilians were killed." He recounted the gruesome details in a quiet monotone.

She squeezed his hand. It didn't take a genius to know that the guilt was eating him up.

He turned away with a small, pained laugh. "Talley and I survived."

Unlacing her fingers, she lifted his hand to her mouth and kissed his massive palm as he had done to her. "And I'm glad you did."

She pressed his palm to her face. Words didn't come easily at painful moments like this, and she had no magic to alleviate the poor man's suffering.

"I could tell you it wasn't your fault, but I know you wouldn't believe me. An evil terrorist killed them, not you. I'm glad that you and Talley survived because I—"

The door slammed open against its hinges, and a thunderous Davis stormed out. Hollie dropped Nick's hand and scurried behind her desk. Her mouth went dry and her lungs froze. An enraged Davis was quite a fearsome spectacle and brought back bad memories best forgotten.

She tried to even her breathing and not cower behind her desk. Nick hadn't stirred from his spot. He watched Davis acting like King Kong as if it were an everyday experience.

Davis blew out a breath and said in an even, calm voice, "Nick, a change in plans. As you might have heard, Grayce will be going alone to see Mrs. Leary in Laurelhurst. She will check in with you on her arrival and departure and maintain phone contact at all times."

Hollie said, "No way."

Davis turned abruptly. "What?"

Nick, unaffected by Davis's fierce entrance, stood up and said in an aggressive voice she had never heard before, "Do not use that tone of voice with Hollie."

The shock on Davis's face was something. His eyes narrowed, and his jaw tightened as he stepped closer to Nick. Oh, shit. Nick's laid-back mood had vanished. All the signs of imminent combat were clear. Nick's spine stiffened as he spread his legs and stuck out his chest. Shit. Shit. Shit. She didn't want them to fight over her.

Davis ran his hands through his black, thick hair. His lips curled into a twist of a smile as he turned toward her. "Nick is right. I shouldn't be taking out my frustration on you."

Transformed from Neolithic to chivalrous in the blink of an eye, Davis looked repentant. "You do a great job taking care of Grayce."

Now she was embarrassed. That was the most considerate thing Davis had ever said to her. She didn't think people got how much she cared for Dr. Walters.

Davis flashed his most endearing smile, the one she knew had charmed the boss when she'd met the fire investigator. "What were you going to tell me?"

"Only that the boss is terrible about her phone. And when she's with animals, she doesn't... She's focused on her work."

Davis breathed deeply, his immense chest moving in and out like a charging bull. "She's promised to communicate. Nick, you'll escort her back and forth to her car after you've inspected it for any tampering. She's taking Mitzi with her as an added precaution."

Davis wasn't taking any chances, but his secret service approach was suffocating the independent doctor.

Davis spoke over his shoulder, his hand on the doorknob. "She expects she'll be two hours at the most. She has promised not to make any stops and will return immediately. I want to know when she is safely back in the office. You can text me upon her arrival. I won't be accessible by phone during the meeting."

CHAPTER SIXTEEN

Nick nodded as Davis repeated his instructions. He was damn glad that Davis had pulled it together, because he didn't want Hollie upset by his punching Davis out. No way would he allow Davis to intimidate Hollie. Not that she'd admit to being scared, but the way her eyes had widened in fear as she'd hid behind her desk was grounds enough for him to do combat.

When Davis left the office, he gave a deep breath of relief. The man was wound so tight he exhausted everyone around him. He could understand why Dr. Walters needed some alone time—a break.

"I thought you two were going to fight." Hollie giggled like a young girl. He wished she could always be vivacious and happy, not all darkness and shadows. "It was like out of a movie, two gladiators fighting to the death." Her snicker made him smile.

He was glad she wasn't upset by what had gone down, but the episode gave him a glimpse of the violence that she must have witnessed from her bastard father and his customers. Meth addicts were unpredictable and dangerous.

The door to Dr. Walters's office opened, and she and Mitzi emerged. "I wanted to make sure you both survived Davis's ground zero mood..." And looking at Hollie, "And that you didn't take it personally."

Nick's affection for the little doc grew immensely. Although she was dealing with a death threat and her boyfriend was going postal, she was caring enough to want to reassure Hollie.

"Mitzi and I are heading to Mrs. Leary's now. I'm sure you've heard all of Davis's stipulations." Her green eyes danced. "This is very hard on all of us, and I appreciate your patience with Davis. I'm hoping that this will be over soon."

"Oh, boss. Don't say that. We all want to keep you safe."

"How could anything happen to me with Davis, Nick, Mitzi, Talley, and you guarding me?" Dr. Walters teased Hollie in a light manner, in no way how she was feeling. "I don't think the president has a bigger or smarter detail. I told Louise Marley that I felt I was the star in one of her spy movies. Louise said Hollywood would never believe that an animal acupuncturist's life could be dangerous."

"They don't know you and your adventures." Hollie laughed, her eyes lightened, and the worry furrow on her forehead relaxed.

"Nick, are you ready to walk me to my car?" Dr. Walters proceeded toward the door, Mitzi following behind. "Hollie, keep looking on the game sites. We need to find Maddy soon, or Davis is going to combust."

"I'm working on it, boss."

"I'll be back for my appointment with Blue and Mr. Gerald."

"Let me go first out the door, Dr. Walters." Nick put Talley's lead on and turned to Hollie. "I'm going to take Talley for a walk before I come back. Do you want anything?"

"No, I'm good. I've got a few ideas to find Earthbro."

CHAPTER SEVENTEEN

With the office finally empty, it was show time. Using Earthbro's sign-in info, Hollie hoped to find a connection on the Warfare site linking Earthbro and Maddy. Hollie's theory was that Maddy was using, and her drug dealers didn't like Angie and the boss getting close to their operation. Hollie hoped to track Maddy through the Warfare forums without alerting her dangerous associates. With Maddy off the streets, Davis and his officials could go after the dealers and whoever had threatened the boss. Now was the time to nail the bastards. The boss looked beat, harried, with the strain of the creeps trying to harm her.

Using Earthbro's hacked info, Hollie signed into his account on the Warfare site. She scrolled through his posts. The dude had achieved a very high level of play—interesting but not helpful.

He spent most of his time in a Sea Monster Guild. He posted as Tegup Frenzy. Weird. Tegup Frenzy had been soliciting people to raid another guild, Portal of Oil. She delved into the chatter.

Unaware of the time, she was stunned when the door to the office opened. Nick and Talley had already finished their walk.

Nick grinned as he walked into the office. "Miss us?"

Hollie stopped typing. "I..."

"Obviously not. You found something and totally forgot about us?"

Shocking how he could read her so well, as if they had known each other for years. She had learned to hide her emotions. She thought of herself as impenetrable to others, but like her with the Warfare firewall, Nick had no trouble hacking right into her.

Releasing Talley from her lead, he walked to stand next to her chair. His musky scent mixed with hot male was familiar and intoxicating.

She tilted her head to look up at him. "How do you do it?"

"Do this?" He leaned down, wrapping his thick hand around her nape. Pulling her close, he took her mouth, angling his head to part her lips, sinking his tongue in, tasting her deeply. He devoured her, his lips and tongue exploring the inside of her mouth.

Her heart did double time, and she panted, trying to catch a breath.

He rubbed his thumb over her lip. "You and I both needed that." His bright eyes had darkened, and his voice was gravelly. He was affected as much by the scorching kiss as she was.

"My kiss make you forget your question?"

His humorous tone snapped her out of her Nick-induced fog. His spontaneous kisses and touches kept her in a sensual haze. Ironically, she was trying to pretend to herself that she didn't like his attention.

"I did find something." She liked the way his eyes filled with warm appreciation.

He rolled a chair next to her. "You hacked Earthbro."

"Yeah. He's a high-level player, and recently he's been posting in an aquatic forum."

"Okay."

"Here's the interesting part. He's been recruiting raiders to help his guild's cause against another guild called Portal of Oil."

Nick listened and watched her with total focus. At first, his intensity had been intimidating, but now his keen interest warmed her.

"I can't find any guild called Portal of Oil," she added.

"Now that is weird. Have others responded to his posts?"

"Yeah, but I haven't had time to read through all the posts."

"I can help track the different posters in his guild." Nick leaned toward the screen.

"Great. Your timing is perfect."

He nudged his solid thigh next to hers. "When we get together, you'll know that my timing..." His voice was rough as he nipped her earlobe.

Heat went through her like a flash fire. Her face and other parts of her body were burning. She could barely get out the words, "Nick, you're making it really hard..."

His laugh rumbled deep in his chest. "That's fair since you're having the same effect on me."

Hollie couldn't help but glance down at Nick's lap. His erection bulged in his tight jeans.

"Looking only makes it worse, honey."

"It does?" This was news to her. She got what men wanted, but she hadn't realized that just looking did it for them.

Nick leaned closer and stroked a tendril of her hair. "Hell, yes. Your interest stirs it all up."

She shifted in her chair as her entire body heated and throbbed in reaction. Everything about Nick was interesting including...

He touched the rim of her ear lightly with the tip of his tongue. "When I'm around you, I'm always fired up and ready."

Prickly chills slithered under her already burning skin as Nick explored her ear with his tongue. "Honey, I've been ready since I met you. Hell, since I saw you in that tight black skirt."

God, he was doing it again. Making her forget, making her want things she wasn't sure she could ever have. She hadn't grown up in a normal family to understand how relationships worked. Nick was the first man she had ever desired. There were a few men who had piqued her interest, but nothing like Nick. And maybe it was time to finally go for it with Nick. But after the mindless, incredible sex he promised with his intense looks and kisses, what then?

He put his hand on the nape of her neck and tugged her so close their breaths mingled. "Don't pull away. Talk to me, honey."

With the flush on his raw-boned face and the way his broad chest heaved under his tight T-shirt, Hollie wanted to crawl onto his lap and do her own exploring. She couldn't look at him without wanting to touch him, kiss him. She shook her head. How had this happened so fast? It was all Nick's fault for being so damned irresistible.

"Nick, I'm not sure this can work."

He lifted her out of the chair as if she weighed nothing and positioned her on his lap. "Oh, honey. I promise you this can work." He nudged her bottom with his erection.

She pushed against his chest. "You idiot. I don't mean the sex..."

He lifted her chin with his knuckles. He searched her face. "Tell me what has you worrying."

"You're hot and heavy now to have sex. But you told me you were interested in more than sex with me, right?"

He raised her hair away from her neck and gently played with the long tendrils. "You know I am. I'll keep telling you over and over again until you believe me. I want to be with you, Hollie. You're the woman for me."

"But that's what I'm saying. I don't know how to do the next part. I assume you'll be good at the sex part. It's the part after, like being normal and dating. My parents weren't exactly sterling examples of how to be in a relationship."

"Honey, you're killing me. It won't be me being good at sex. It will be you and me coming together. And it will be more than good. It will be fantastic, mind-blowing, making each other happy."

Nick made it sound easy. It couldn't be that easy or she wouldn't be so frightened.

He ran his hands up and down her arms. "I want to make you happy. Don't you want to make me happy?"

She chewed on her lower lip. She did want to make Nick happy. She did enjoy making the people she cared about happy. "I think so."

He chuckled. "Guess that's a start." His hand brushed her neck and along her cheeks. "You're a very loving and compassionate woman who cares about a lot of people. I don't think we're going to have a problem caring for each other."

Hollie wanted to believe Nick. "Let's not sweat it now. We need to get this business with Dr. Walters straightened out, and then we can figure out the rest. Right?"

She tried to jump off of Nick's lap. "You're right. I'm focused on finding Maddy."

His hands went around her waist and pulled her back against his chest. "Hold on there, partner," he whispered against her ear. "Before we get down..." His hot breath against her neck and her ear caused shivers to race along her already sensitive skin. "Let's have dinner tonight. I'll cook for you at my new place."

Hollie shook her head. She wouldn't turn and look at him, because she wouldn't be able to say no.

His hands were wandering from her waist upward, right underneath her breasts. "No seduction. I promise. Only dinner and a whole lot of kissing and touching. Does that work for you?"

She tried to pull away, get out of his lap, but his hands tightened. "Hey, you okay?"

She nodded without looking back. She didn't want to see his triumphant look.

He released her. "Great. Now let's nail Earthbro."

CHAPTER EIGHTEEN

———————————

ollie jumped out of his lap. And Nick felt the void
without her warm body nestled next to him. She didn't
show any outward sign of loss. She went immediately
back to her computer, and her fingers flew over the keyboard.

He stood to get his laptop, glad for Hollie's distraction since he
didn't need to call attention to his jones. With his back to her, he bent
over to reach his gear he had stuffed underneath the chair.

"What's Earthbro's character's name?"

"Tegup Frenzy." Hollie didn't look up. "We need to sort through
all the posts on the forums he's entered to see if Maddy has
responded."

He pulled a chair around in front of Hollie's desk to face her.
With the shelves and a cupboard behind her desk, there wasn't
enough room for the two of them to work next to each other. He
missed being able to touch her, but he had tonight. He couldn't
believe she had agreed to his dinner plans. He'd expected that she'd
fight him.

He had moved to his friend's place on Lake Washington, to be
closer and available to do guard duty for Dr. Walters. One of his

college buddies owned a rental in the north end of Seattle. It was perfect for him and Talley since they could both swim each day and pursue Hollie. Since the move, he'd been fixated on how to lure Hollie to his place, and tonight it was happening.

Hollie gazed up from the computer, catching him in his moment of fantasizing.

"I thought you said you were going to help."

"Yes, sir." He couldn't stop his grin. She was one bossy woman. His woman. He had started to think of her that way. Not that she was ready to consider all of his plans.

Hollie stretched her neck and back against her chair, thrusting her breasts forward in the little tank top she wore, paired with a long, clinging skirt. For someone who had been exposed to men's baser ways, she really was innocent on how men's minds worked. If he thought she'd be amenable, he'd leap over the desk to get to those delectable prizes she presented.

She caught him gawking at her body again. She rolled her eyes. "Really? Nick, focus."

"Yes, ma'am. Can you tell me when Earthbro started posting? I'll start there."

"He has been posting on fifteen forums for over two years."

"But we've been searching all the forums and haven't found him."

"Exactly, but with his sign-in info, I can track which ones he's been on most recently. His newest and favorite is the Sea Monster Forum."

Nick went straight to the Sea Monster forum. "Shit. There were over four hundred posts."

"But Maddy has only been missing two months. You start at July, and I'll start in August."

"Sounds like a plan." He scrolled back to July and began to read the comments. On the third page down, he found a character named madwomanmollusk.

"Hollie, I might have something."

Her eyes widened. "Really?"

MEN UNDER FIRE   103

"There is a character named madwomanmollusk."

She jumped out of her seat and came around to his side of the desk. "Angie told the boss that Maddy had a lot of anger." She leaned over him to look closer at his screen. He got a whiff of lemon shampoo and flowery Hollie. It took all his self-control not to pull her back down onto his lap again.

"I can search Earthbro's account to see if he posted to madwomanmollusk." She went back to her computer. Within minutes, she shouted, "Holy shit! I've hit the mother lode."

Now it was Nick's turn to jump out of his chair.

"Earthbro sent out this message last night to madwomanmollusk and ten other players about a sale on his T-shirt website." Hollie pointed to the website. "It's happening. One bang of a sale. Today from twelve noon to two p.m. This is happening today. And look at the awful T-shirt closely." She enlarged the screen to enhance the front of the shirt. And then stood up to enable him to sit down.

Nick peered closely. The white T-shirt depicted an explosion on Seattle's waterfront. The sky was filled with ominous dark smoke, and the buildings were engulfed in flames. Positioned behind the Ferris wheel, a tanker with the name *Tegup Frenzy* sank into a black oil slick, and people ran from a blown-up, crumbling Pier 69.

"Oh, my God. Is this part of the game, or is he going to blow up the pier?" Nick asked.

"How can we find out?" Hollie stretched to look closer at the screen. "He's got his character's name on the tanker. What does Tegup stand for?"

Nick shook his head. "I've no idea. It's not the name of an Indian tribe, is it?"

Hollie kept staring at the screen, trying to decipher the word. She laughed out loud. "It's Puget spelled backwards. Puget Frenzy."

"You're right. This could all be part of a guild."

Hollie's shoulders slumped. "What can we do?"

Nick stood and pulled her chair out for her to sit. "We should look at the response from his post and see if madwomanmollusk commented about the T-shirt sale."

Hollie started typing. "That's a brilliant idea. I'm on it."

He smiled down at her, but her focus was on the screen. "Madwomenmollusk's comment was, 'Rad shirt. Definitely need one.'"

Hollie read all ten comments aloud to him. "They agree to buy the T-shirt. We just don't know if that's a code for something real or they are buying his shirt."

Hollie scooted closer to the desk. "I'm going to look up if there are any events on the waterfront today."

"Look specifically at Pier 69," he added.

Hollie twisted her neck to stare up at him. "You know, you're really good at this."

He kissed her lightly on the forehead, then the nose. "We're really good together."

Her eyes flickered with emotion, and her lips curved into a tentative smile. "You might be right."

Nick's lungs constricted, and his body twitched in readiness. He wanted to take her into his arms and show her exactly how good they were together. Carnal images flickered across his brain.

"Oh, my God." Hollie's shout interrupted his erotic fantasy. "There is a port commissioner's meeting today from twelve to two p.m. And guess what's on the agenda?"

"Oil tankers in Puget Sound."

"How did you know?"

"The T-shirt and the fact that there has been endless news coverage around the danger of the oil trains and the possibility of increased oil spills in Puget Sound."

Hollie cracked her knuckles, a habit he recognized when she was anxious or unsure. "But this could all be part of the game and only fictional."

Nick couldn't buy that this newest discovery was only part of extended Warfare game-playing. There were too many coincidences

—the threat needed to be assessed. At this point, he wasn't quite ready to alert the FBI and police department's bomb squad.

His gut was reacting, and he trusted his instincts. He and Talley had survived four years of deployment because of his instincts, but he didn't want Hollie involved in any danger.

"This warrants looking into. Call Angie and ask if she can meet Talley and me down on Pier 69 to see if Maddy might show. Whether there is a real bomb threat, I'm not sure."

Hollie stood up. Her chest puffed up in outrage. "You and Talley? What about me?"

He should've known Hollie would never accept his plan. "Honey, don't you have to stay in the office?"

She strutted around her desk, and he wanted to grab and kiss her, but he valued his boys too much. "Nick Welby, don't you dare honey me in a condescending voice. And don't you need to be here when Dr. Walters gets back?"

He hadn't forgotten his first duty. "I'll be back in time for the doc's arrival. She said she wouldn't be back for two hours. I can get to the waterfront and back before she gets here."

"I'm going with you." She stood toe-to-toe with him, except she had on flimsy sandals. For a horny man, this face-off wasn't exactly confrontational with her pink toenails and her luscious chest expanded.

He tucked her errant curl behind her ear. "But if it's a real threat, it could be dangerous. And Hollie, I couldn't let anything happen to you."

Hollie stood on tiptoe and brushed his hair away from his forehead. "I feel the same, Nick. I can't let you and Talley go into danger without me." And for the first time, Hollie initiated a kiss—a sweet, erotic kiss. She used her tongue to outline his lower lip before she gave a little love bite. "Remember what you said. We're good together."

Aroused and amused, he chuckled as he pulled her against his chest. "You know, you don't fight fair."

Hollie wrapped her hands around his neck. "This doesn't feel like fighting." She rubbed her sweet, soft body against his.

"Okay, okay. You win."

Her eyes were twinkling in devilish pride. He loved seeing her playful. She laughed a husky laugh, deep in her chest. He felt her warm, lush body against him. He lifted her off her feet and kissed her hard, his mouth covering hers, demonstrating his need to mark her as his. He groaned. "Let's go. You can call Angie from my truck."

No way did he plan to allow Hollie near any danger. He'd lock her in his truck if he had to, but hopefully she'd be sensible and realize he was in charge.

CHAPTER NINETEEN

Hollie, Nick, and Talley walked toward Pier 69. Although Nick held her hand, he had set her at a distance. Since he had parked his truck, his whole demeanor, stance, and mood had altered. No leering looks, no playful touches, no sexy smiles. He and Talley were locked on the mission.

During the drive from Fremont, he'd been distracted. As if mentally scrolling through all the possible horrendous scenarios. His hand had rested on her thigh. Periodically, he'd looked over to check on her and then gently squeezed her thigh.

Nick parked the car beyond the sculpture garden. As they walked down the hill to Pier 69, Nick's pace quickened, and she almost had to run to keep up. It was a sunny day, and the water shimmered on Puget Sound. Since this was the height of summer, the sidewalks were crammed with tourists and families. Nick's eyes darted back and forth as he scanned the entire area.

They waited at the red light to cross the train tracks and the street. Nick dropped her hand, turned toward her, and grasped her shoulders. "I don't want you to say a word, honey. Just listen." His voice had a tone of authority she had never heard before.

Hollie's heart raced, and her stomach fluttered in response to the grave look on his face. "Got it."

"Before we go into the building, I have to know that you'll do exactly as I tell you. Can you promise to follow my instructions? No hesitation. No questions asked."

She tried to pull away, but he tightened his grip. "You're asking a lot, Nick. Do you really believe that the T-shirt is a real threat?"

He hesitated. "I don't know. But I have to assume the worst. And I can't be distracted by trying to protect you."

She leveled her badass look at him. "I can protect myself."

He exhaled, blowing the air slowly through his lips. "I knew this was a bad idea. I should've left you at the office."

Hollie snarled. "Left me at the office! Like you had a choice?"

The light changed, and the other people started to cross, but Nick wouldn't let her go. He stared at her, no longer the intense male-to-female look, now a male imposing his will.

Hollie examined his face, searching for the tender man. The change was dramatic. His face was clenched in stress. His angular jaw had clamped down, and the little crinkles around his eyes strained.

He looked the same as the first day he had come to the office. He was reliving Afghanistan, surrounded by danger, trying to protect her. How could she not recognize the stress and bravery of this man in facing this possible threat? He was unlike any man she had ever met. She couldn't possibly cause him any further distress. She rubbed her hand over his tight chest. "Okay, Nick. I'll do what you tell me. I won't fight you on anything."

His mouth opened and closed, then he gave her a quick busk on her lips. "Thank you. I know how hard that was for you."

He took her elbow to cross the street. "Angie is going to meet us in front of the building, right?"

"She said she'd wait outside like you asked."

"And you left a message for Dr. Walters that we'd meet her back in the office, right?"

"You were in the car when I made the phone calls."

"Sorry, but once Talley and I start working, I have to know all the other details are in place."

Nick was preparing for every contingency. His square, defiant chin was tucked tight; his neck and shoulders were pulled back in the erect military bearing. The man looked like a well-trained soldier, nothing like the flirty man hitting on her in the office. Tension vibrated off of him, and she found herself mirroring the same. Her heart palpitated, and her mouth suddenly went dry.

They could be walking into a potentially lethal situation. This palpable fear of the unknown and weight of the responsibility to uncover and stop the violence was exactly what Nick and Talley had gone through every day of their deployment. She touched his arm. "I'm sorry I got you and Talley into this mess."

His eyes were directed ahead, scanning every movement. "Talley and I are used to messes."

She kept quiet. She felt a bit hurt by his abrupt answer, but she wouldn't distract him. She kept wondering if he considered her part of the mess.

She gave herself a good talking-to. This wasn't about her or her fragile feelings. They were here to help the boss and find Maddy. Hopefully Angie, who she had never met but had seen in pictures, had arrived.

By the front door was a woman hidden in the shadows, dressed in military fatigue pants and a white T-shirt. She had long black hair held in a braid.

"I see Angie. Or I think it's Angie."

Nick grunted.

Angie stepped out of the shadows when they neared. "Sgt. Welby, Hollie?"

Angie carried the same intense, upright stiffness of Nick. Angie also was a beautiful woman. She had high cheekbones, big, round eyes, and the lips of a super model. And if she didn't hold herself like a surfboard, she could grace any *Sports Illustrated* swimsuit cover.

Hollie looked up to see if Nick was noticing. Of course he was. Nick was a very sexy man, meeting a hot woman.

Definitely Nick was looking at Angie when he spoke to her. "We might have brought you down for nothing."

"I'm aware of the situation, sir. I appreciate your effort in trying to find my friend and fellow Marine."

"Because of the small possibility of a bomb threat, once my dog and I start working, I'll need you to be point. If it's necessary, can you keep everyone calm and get the people out of and away from the building?"

"Yes, sir."

"I'm only planning for worst-case scenario since we really don't have any evidence that this is more than a gaming group. But if your friend is part of the threat, are you prepared to handle her?"

"Sir, Maddy and I served two tours together. She isn't part of this. I'd stake my life on her."

Nick smiled warmly at Angie. "Leave no Marine behind."

"Yes, sir. Oorah!"

Hollie tried to ignore the dark hole of jealousy and envy gnawing at her insides as she watched Nick treat Angie as an equal. She should be grateful he hadn't given Angie his sexy, full-electric smile. He treated Angie like a fellow soldier, and she couldn't fault him. Hollie hadn't served. She'd done nothing brave or courageous like these two wounded veterans. She wished she didn't feel left out and alone.

Nick turned toward her. "Hollie, your job is to run out of the building and call the bomb squad. Move as far away from the building as you can and then call."

Outrage stiffened her spine, but her voice quivered in hurt. "I'm going to run out and leave you, Talley, and all the people behind?"

Nick seemed to grow bigger and taller before her eyes, dominating her with his force. His eyes were icy and his voice steely. "Yes, time will be of the essence to notify the bomb squad."

She started to argue and saw the glimpse of fear in his eyes before he hardened his tone. "Can you carry out your job, or do you want to wait outside?"

Hollie wanted to say more to Nick, to tell him how hard it'd be to leave him. And how much she had come to care, but with Angie listening, she bowed her head to hide her fear and hurt. "I'll do whatever you need, Nick."

CHAPTER TWENTY

Grayce Walters kept her gaze on the road ahead, but out of the corner of her eye, she observed her captor. The man who'd abducted her in the middle of the afternoon in the fancy Laurelhurst neighborhood. He looked like a regular guy, calm and in control, but she sensed his frenetic energy and how easily he could snap.

"I won't ask again. Now talk," he commanded.

"I was searching for a missing woman on Beacon Hill."

"There's more to it." He leaned over to take her finger and waited.

Her entire body tightened in expectation of the approaching pain. "I was helping a client find her friend. That's all it was. Nothing else."

"Don't try to placate me." He dropped her hand. "You're just like her—always smoothing, always pretending."

At first, Grayce thought she could reason with him. Now, she realized he was both delusional and paranoid. "Are you talking about Maddy?"

"You can't stop, can you? Picking and prodding. Always trying to get everyone to do what you want. You're not going to manage me like my mother." He gripped the steering wheel tightly. His dark eyes had a strange blaze, as if he was in his own world that was ready to explode.

"I'm sorry. I didn't mean to upset you." Her voice had become soft and soothing, the same voice she used when she was wary of an unpredictable animal.

"My God, you talk like her. Looking down your nose on those of us who don't measure up to your superior standards. But today you're going to be looking from my perch."

Her heart struck sharp blows against her chest.

"You're gonna get to look down on the whole city from the park."

He needed Grayce to be part of playing out his fantasy. He wanted her to be impressed by his plan. In some weird, twisted way, he equated her with his mother.

"I'm not familiar with Jack Block Park, but I'm sure the views are spectacular." She had succeeded with an out-of-control, vicious sun bear at the zoo. She could handle this obsessed, mentally ill man.

"How do you know where we're going?" His body stiffened, ready to strike.

She had made a huge mistake. Animals were much easier than people.

"Bitch, how do you know that we are going to Jack Block Park? Who else knows?" he exploded, his face red with rage, the veins bulging on his neck.

Grayce detected his musky smell, that of a cornered animal. "When you turned off at Alki, I knew what park we were going to. There are no other parks at this exit."

He drove and turned in front of the large park sign partially obscured by trees and bushes. They crossed railroad tracks. He stopped the car partway down, hidden from the traffic, on the access road to the park.

"You just said you weren't familiar with Jack Block Park."

His ominous calm was more frightening than his rage.

"I've never been to the park, but I know of its existence. I grew up in Seattle."

"For lying to me, your stupid dog is going to pay."

He dialed Gator. "Put your phone on speaker. And kick the dog in the head. I want Dr. Walters to hear the poodle suffer."

"No, please. I'll tell you. Don't hurt Mitzi," she pleaded desperately. "I found a map of Jack Block Park in a sleeping bag."

His breathing deepened into aggressive surges. "You went through my sleeping bag?"

Never show your fear to a cornered animal. Fear breeds fear.

"We didn't know it was yours, and we were hoping it belonged to Maddy."

"Gator, kick the dog."

Mitzi gave a keening cry that tore away all shreds of Grayce's composure.

"Brandon, do you want me to do it again?" Gator's humored voice thundered in the car.

His name was Brandon. She searched her mind but didn't remember meeting him.

"That's all for now." He turned toward Grayce. "Gator loves his job."

His smile was toothy and fiendish. She would have remembered someone so cruel. She had never met him. He never planned to release Mitzi. She had to escape. He had used

the devoted poodle to trap Grayce in his sick game.

CHAPTER TWENTY-ONE

With an eager Talley at his side, Nick escorted Hollie and Angie into the newly remodeled glass-and-steel Pier 69, home to the Port of Seattle offices and boat terminal for passenger service between Seattle and Victoria, British Columbia.

He kept a firm grip on Talley's lead. The dog was ready to play the game of find the scent. Nick's heart slammed sharp blows inside his chest. He could barely hear above the roaring pulse in his ears. This had all the potential of one major clusterfuck. Since the discovery of the T-shirt, he'd tried to calculate the risks, as he'd been trained to do. Pier 69 was the perfect location to make a violent statement. International travelers, tourists, and the port commissioners all in one location.

Logic told him the T-shirt lead was weak and the risks slim that a gamer had the balls to blow up Pier 69. Gamers lived in a world of fantasy. If that were true, why did his gut burn like he had Montezuma's revenge and his entire body shake?

He played and replayed each scenario. His answer gave no satisfaction—either pursuing gamers was a stupid waste of time or he was making a big mistake by bringing Hollie into danger.

Arrow signs were posted on the wall pointing the direction to the port commissioners' meeting. As they came around the corner, a large group of people congregated, waiting to gain entry into the meeting. Shit. Could it possibly be any worse—a large crowd in a very confined space with only two hallways to exit?

There were no security guards or bag checks for those attending the public meeting. As he got closer, hell, yeah, it got worse. Half of the crowd were young and carried backpacks. His assumption that the gamer group would be college punks and would stand out in an older, civic-minded group was gone.

He scrutinized the crowd for anyone who stood out or appeared nervous. Two women in their twenties, both with heavy backpacks, stood together. One woman, short and plump, kept looking over her shoulder. Her eyes darted back and forth as she chewed on her nails. Memories of the woman in Kabul, running toward his platoon, flashed through his brain. Waves of heat and ice chased over every inch of his skin as if he were back under the desert heat. He shook his head and his shoulders as if he could shake away the horrific memory.

To clear his head, he glanced down at Hollie. Her face was pale and strained. He hated to see her fearful. He wanted to hold her and kiss the worry away. He couldn't let her distract him from the mission. Clear focus was the only way to ensure her safety.

He whispered to Hollie, "Honey, stay here. Talley and I are going to walk through the crowd."

Hollie's face shot up to his. She gave a little gasp before she swallowed against whatever protest she wanted to say. "Okay, Nick. I'll wait here."

He nodded toward Angie, who stepped away from Hollie and slowly followed behind him.

Nick bent to Talley, keen for the chance to work. With the promise of a game of ball after she found the scent, she strained with excitement to detect the scent of explosives. He gave the command. "Talley, search."

Nick directed Talley toward the two women. His breathing accelerated, and his mouth went dry as his body went into hyper-drive. The adrenaline surged, priming his body for action and his mind into precise focus. Every one of his senses was heightened. His heart beat a fast tattoo, a rhythm that owed nothing to exertion and everything to pure adrenaline rush.

The plump woman jolted backward, acting as if she was ready to run. Her friend put her hand on her arm to restrain her. Nick kept his eyes on her as he walked directly toward her. He wasn't above using intimidation as a tactic. He was a pretty scary guy when pumped up.

Her friend was talking frantically. The woman shook her head, then put her hands up as if surrendering.

They were within ten feet of the woman when Talley alerted. Talley lurched forward on her lead toward the nervous woman. With Nick and Angie bearing down, the woman turned and tore down the adjacent hallway. For someone hefty, the girl could run. She sprinted toward the outside door. Fear of capture was an incredible physical incentive.

Nick and Talley had to negotiate around the crowd before they burst into a sprint. If she were Earthbro, she wouldn't be running away from the crowd. As he gained on the chunky girl, Nick expected that she would drop her backpack and take off. He wasn't convinced this woman was a bomber, but Talley started to whine as they gained on her.

Nick shouted, "Stop. Now!" He was prepared to tackle her, but he'd prefer not.

The young woman turned around. Her face was bright red and her breathing winded from the exertion.

She stopped. "I didn't do anything. I was only going to take pictures."

Angie was right behind them.

The woman bent over to catch her breath, clearly out of shape from her little run.

Talley strained closer to the woman and sat, her signal that she had found the explosives.

Terror gushed from his pores. The flood of fear and adrenaline brought lucidity and hyper-awareness and the familiar chemical taste on his tongue. "Good work, Talley."

The dog thumped her tail, ready for the reward. He wished he shared his dog's enthusiasm for discovering explosives.

He took slow, measured breaths and switched gears to his well-entrenched training. This wasn't his first rodeo. But hope to God, his last.

As trained, Talley didn't move but maintained her point.

Nick turned to Angie and spoke. His calm voice echoed in his head and the empty hallway. "Call the bomb squad. Clear the building. And get Hollie out of here."

The red-faced girl started to shake. "I don't have a bomb. I've got my camera in the backpack."

Nick's mind raced through all the scenarios in seconds—best to leave the backpack in the empty hallway than take it out to the streets. He hoped Angie cleared the building quickly.

Nick said in a measured voice, "Slowly take off your backpack and place it on the ground."

She swung the backpack from her shoulder. He scrutinized her hands on the pack. Was there a mechanism to pull, or was someone else from a distance to detonate the bomb?

"Easy." Nick kept eye contact with the woman, his voice low and controlled.

"I swear I don't have a bomb in my backpack. I was going to film the demonstration. We were going to throw oil on the port commissioners. That's all. No bombs. We're not that kind of group."

Her adamant claim that she didn't have a bomb didn't add up. "What about Earthbro's T-shirt? That didn't look like a peaceful demonstration."

"That's Brandon, a guy in our group. He's really into drawing explosions and shit, but none of us are violent."

She wasn't acting like a suicide bomber, ready to kill hundreds of people. She had no signs of resignation and defeat that he had seen on the suicide bombers' faces. But who could really tell which people had the need to destroy themselves and take others with them? "My dog says there is a bomb in your backpack, and she is never wrong."

She jerked in place.

"Slowly and calmly put the bomb on the ground. No fast movements and no jerking."

She held her body stiff. "I'm telling you I don't have a bomb. We came today to protest the oil tankers. We aren't violent."

"How is the bomb rigged? Is it to detonate when someone opens your backpack?"

"I don't know," she sobbed as tears ran down her face. "I don't know anything about a bomb."

Nick kept his focus on her hands. She truly didn't seem to know about the explosives. But he didn't trust anyone in these deadly circumstances. He trusted no one but his dog.

The girl's red face was now a deathly white. Her hands shook as she gingerly lowered the backpack to the cement floor.

Talley sat waiting as if this entire drama was part of an entertaining game.

Nick pulled on Talley's lead to get away from the bomb. "Let's go, girl."

An excited Talley pranced next to him as he walked around the backpack. He grabbed the girl's elbow and moved them quickly toward the outside door facing Alaskan Way. He prayed Hollie was far away from the building.

CHAPTER TWENTY-TWO

Hollie stood suspended, unable to move, as if she were floating in a bad dream. Nick and Talley chased a woman with a backpack down a hallway, and she stood frozen.

Every instinct urged her to run after Nick and the woman. But she had promised Nick to remain in this spot, and her word meant something. Her parents had never honored anything except their next deal and their next high. Hollie kept her promises.

Like the huddled crowd, she waited and stared down the hallway where Nick and Talley had disappeared. In less than a few minutes, Angie ran back to the crowd and said in a low, commanding voice, "I need you to clear the building now." One kid started to protest, but Angie leveled him with one look. "I said now!"

Indecision and gut-wrenching fear kept Hollie motionless. Angie raced over, her tone sharp. "Hollie, get out of here. Move as far away as you can from this building. Do you understand?"

"What's going on?"

Angie lowered her voice. "Nick and his dog found a bomb."

"I'm supposed to call the bomb squad."

"I already called them." Angie pointed to the door. "You need to get the hell out of here."

Hollie couldn't do nothing. "I can help."

Already focused on the crowd, Angie turned and stopped. "No, you need to get out of here. It was Nick's last instruction before I left him."

Hollie couldn't breathe; for the first time in her life, she might faint. Although she was upright, she had the overwhelming feeling of falling into emptiness. "But what about Nick and Talley?"

Angie grabbed her arm and pushed her toward the door. "Get going now. Let Nick do his job."

And with that command, Angie sprinted toward the meeting room.

She couldn't leave Nick and Talley. She thought of Nick's face when he'd asked her to promise. Her heart thudded, and she was abruptly cold with dread, nauseated from it. If anything happened to him... Wavering, she ran to the door. She had to trust Nick and believe.

She ran outside into the bright sunlight. Mayhem had already broken loose. Sirens screamed as fire trucks and police cars rushed from both ways on Alaskan Way toward Pier 69. Two helicopters hovered. A patrol car careened around the corner of Broad Street and drove up the curb. The officers, with their guns drawn, jumped out of their vehicle.

With all the focus on Pier 69, no one paid her any attention when she crossed the street and walked toward the entrance where she assumed Nick and Talley would exit. She wouldn't think about any other possibility.

She wasn't moving any farther away from the building until she saw him come out.

Two Seattle Police vans blocked her view. The swat team, armed with rifles, poured out of the van. The other had its doors open. Two men suited up in garb straight out of Star Wars with thick, puffy suits, high collars, and helmets. Swat and bomb teams were on the scene to protect Nick and Talley.

She watched all the boat passengers filing out of the other side of Pier 69, the ingress for the ferries to Canada. She would not move until she saw Nick. As the swat officers spread out and surrounded the building, there was an opening in the convoy of vans, fire trucks, patrol cars. She scanned the group of responders and spotted Nick in his black T-shirt.

Relief made her weak in the knees. He was safe. Thank the Lord. Although she hadn't prayed in years, she whispered a prayer of thanks. She couldn't imagine what she would do if anything happened to Nick.

Nick spoke with a bulky police officer. Although his back was to her, a rush of tenderness filled her at the way he gestured and the familiar tilt to his head. How had she become so attached to him and his dog?

The girl he'd chased was in handcuffs, and another police officer held on to her elbow. None of the officers were scurrying out of harm's way. Had they already decided that the explosion wasn't imminent?

Should she call Nick and tell him where she was? He would have to answer a lot of questions, and she didn't want to interrupt. She cracked her knuckles, trying to decide how to proceed. It wasn't every day she had to cope with a bomb threat. She wanted to laugh and cry at the same time. She could've used James's warped sense of humor about now.

Oh, shit. What about the boss? Nick was supposed to be back at the office, but he definitely was needed here. Davis was going to be pissed if the boss was left unprotected. She'd better call the boss and tell her they might be delayed. Since she'd come in Nick's truck, she had no way of getting back to the office to guard the boss. And it sure didn't look like an Uber would be able to get down here.

She called the boss's cell. The phone went to voice mail. It was typical for the boss not to answer if she was involved with a patient. And then she dialed the office phone to check messages and also check if the boss had gotten back. She doubted the boss would hurry through her visit. She always took her time with Mrs. Leary.

Hollie left a message for the boss on the office voice mail and her cell to cover all bases. She looked up from her phone, and Nick and Talley were crossing the street toward her. The sight of Nick and his dog made her stomach drop and flip like an upside-down ride at the Puyallup Fair.

Hollie gulped. She wanted to run to him and throw herself into his arms. The intensity of her feelings stunned her. His courage and bravery had in her awe and a bit overwhelmed.

She ran her hands along her skirt to prevent herself from touching him. "Oh, Nick... I didn't know if I should call you or what."

He gave her the smile that melted her into a heap. "I spotted you crossing the street, but I couldn't leave. How you holding up?"

Hollie was glad for his cool manner. If he showed any sympathy or concern, she'd be bawling like a baby. And she never cried. Never. "I'm good."

Nick examined her face. "Good, huh?"

She wasn't sure if Nick saw her fear. "The bomb isn't going to blow up?"

"They're taking the threat very seriously especially with passengers arriving and departing to Canada. But with the amount of time that's passed and jostling that the backpack received and the fact that none of us are convinced Teresa has the makings of a bomber, the risk has been lowered, but they're following protocol."

She felt awkward and unsure. She bent down and rubbed Talley's head. "You were amazing."

"Talley is pretty amazing." He grasped her by her arms and pulled her against his chest. "But what about her handler? Do you think he's amazing?"

The warmth and security of his arms were too much. All the feelings she had worked so hard to control came flooding out. "Nick, I think you're more than amazing."

She wrapped her arms around his waist and talked into his chest. "I never, ever want to have to watch you and Talley walk into danger again. It was the worst moment of my life, I swear, Nick. You can never leave me like that again."

She squeezed him tight, holding on to the safety of his heat and strength.

"I'm not planning on leaving you."

She looked up and got snared in his loving look. Did he mean what she thought?

He pushed the hair back from her eyes. "It's not going to be easy to forget that I brought you down here into danger."

"Nick, I was coming no matter what. And you're never going to leave me behind. Do you hear me?"

He sprinkled light kisses along her face. "Is that right, honey?"

She stepped back and gave her scary *don't mess with me* look. "Damn right. Do you know how hard it was to not help you?"

He played with her hair, twisting and smoothing the curls. "Angie told me that you wanted to stay. Thank you for keeping your promise, honey."

"I'd never break a promise to you, Nick." Hollie gulped. She wanted to say more, but she was cautious and unsure. She had never felt this way before and had no idea how to tell Nick she cared.

"About promises, I'm worried about getting back to meet Dr. Walters. I'm going to be debriefed by everyone. Police, FBI, Homeland Security."

"I already left a message that we're going to be late. I didn't tell her why. I didn't want to worry her with everything else going on. You don't think the bomb is related to the threat against the boss, do you?"

"I'm not sure, but I'm not going to take a chance. I called Davis, but he didn't pick up. Can you keep trying to call him? I'm not sure I'll have a chance. I've got to get back. Can you do me a favor?"

"Anything."

"Can you take Talley and stay here? I want to be able to see you while they're questioning me. I want to know you're safe. It will mean a lot."

No one had ever cared for her like Nick. A deep sense of security curled around her heart. He wanted to make sure that she and Talley remained safe.

"Our handler wants us both to stay, Talley." She had almost said *as girlfriend and dog*, but caught herself.

Nick did a deep belly laugh. She felt the movement of his broad chest against her. "Trust me, honey. I've never thought of you in the way I think of Talley."

At the promise in his seductive look and his lowered voice, Hollie wanted him to follow through right here and now. She was ready.

"I'll be here waiting for you, Nick."

Holding her face between his hands, he took her mouth in a kiss that started slow but quickly turned into a deep, soft promise.

CHAPTER TWENTY-THREE

Nick dodged the crowds milling around on Alaskan Way to return for questioning by Seattle's police and, judging by the three black SUVs, the FBI. As people shoved and pushed, he realized he was alert and focused but not hypervigilant.

All the same elements—noise, crowds, stress—were here, but he wasn't reacting to the overload. Part of the difference was that he and Talley had been back at work. But the bigger reason was the woman waiting across the street with his dog.

With Hollie's presence, he felt a deep and real calm. Knowing she waited for him took off the edge. He wanted her always there.

Did she feel the same? Tonight he'd find out.

He turned back to catch a glimpse of Hollie. He wanted to get her away from all this madness, away from the disturbing side of humanity. For someone who came from a shitty family, she was one sweet, loving woman. Her tough-girl act was endearing, especially when she was feeling her most vulnerable.

An FBI agent with the trademark vest and jacket approached him. Tall and confident of his place in the scheme of this scenario, he offered his hand. "Sgt. Welby. You and your dog saved a lot of lives today. The bomb had enough RDX to blow up half of the waterfront."

Nick swallowed hard against the anxiety seeping up his gut into his throat. What the hell? He hadn't doubted Talley's nose, but he'd started to have misgivings when the police had questioned the credibility of the Warfare connection and Teresa's genuine shock about her backpack.

He twisted to check on Hollie. He couldn't think of all the possible what-ifs. They would all come to haunt him in the middle of the night. "The bomb has been disabled?"

"Yes, all is safe for the moment, until we understand the threat. I need to hear all the details of why you were on site."

"Yes, of course." Nick had a feeling this was going to take a while. He shouldn't have asked Hollie to wait on the street. But he needed to be able to see her, to know she was safe and close by if he needed to get to her.

Thirty minutes of endless questioning by the FBI, and Nick was finished. He gave Hollie a thumbs-up sign that he was ready to leave. He started to cross the street when he heard his name shouted.

Angie and another woman were behind him and signaling for him to stop. Hell, he had totally forgotten about Angie and where she had disappeared to when everything had gone down.

"Sgt. Welby, wait up." Angie and the woman followed him across the street. Hollie had spotted Angie and came forward with Talley.

For a veteran suffering from PTSD, Angie didn't look as if the stress of the day had gotten to her. She had a wide-ass grin.

"Hollie and Sgt. Welby, I want you to meet Maddy."

A short, attractive blond woman spoke to Hollie. "It is great to finally meet you. Angie explained how you and Dr. Walters have gone to great lengths to search for Angie and me. I can't tell you how grateful I am for your efforts."

Hollie's widened eyes and the restless way she shifted her weight back and forth were signs that she was as shocked as he was to find Maddy to be a well-spoken woman and not a strung-out druggie.

"I'm confused." Hollie looked to Nick.

He shrugged his shoulders. He hadn't a clue.

"Of course you are, as is Angie. I can't explain everything, but I've been working undercover."

Hollie gasped. "What the f—?" She caught herself. Nick agreed with Hollie's take. This whole state of affairs was getting too convoluted and bizarre.

Right then, Nick's phone rang. He checked the ID. It was Davis.

Nick turned toward Maddy. "This is Davis, Dr. Walters's boyfriend. There have been threats against Dr. Walters's life, which might be connected to her search for the two of you and possibly your undercover work."

Neither woman seemed surprised by this news. He stepped around the women and stood next to Hollie. He needed her close by. Hollie leaned into his side. "I'm going to put him on speaker."

Nick tried to focus on the next problem. It was turning into one hell of a day, "Davis, I've been trying to reach you."

"Nick, what the fuck? Why haven't you answered?"

"We've got a situation, sir." Nick tried for calm since obviously Davis hadn't toned down since the last confrontation.

"What the hell does that mean?" Yeah, Davis definitely wasn't chill.

Nick summarized the day's events. "There was a bomb down on Pier 69, set to blow up the port commissioner's meeting."

"How the hell would you know that?"

"Hollie and I discovered in the World of Warfare chat room that something big was going to happen, so we came down here with Angie. Talley discovered the bomb."

"Where is Grayce?" Davis's voice got rougher and louder.

"We've been trying to call her at Mrs. Leary's to tell her about the meeting and that we were leaving the office. She hasn't picked up. Hollie said she's terrible about answering her phone. We've been calling her for the last hour. She should be finished with her visit by now. I then tried to call you, sir. And you didn't answer. And since we got down here, all hell has

broken loose. The bomb squad is here right now."

"Where is Grayce?"

"I don't know, sir. Hollie wants to speak with you."

"Davis." Hollie's voice was tremulous, the tough-ass street kid long gone.

Nick was unnerved by the dramatic change in her.

"She isn't answering her phone, but we assumed she was still with Mrs. Leary. We were heading back to the office, but Nick had to be interviewed by the FBI."

"Give me Mrs. Leary's number."

"I don't have the number with me. I know we were supposed to guard Grayce, but I thought she was fine. Now, I'm afraid something happened to her with all the craziness here."

"Calm down, Hollie," Davis shouted over the phone, obviously not following his own advice.

Maddy touched Hollie's elbow. "I've news on Dr. Walters's whereabouts."

Angie, Hollie, and he turned to Maddy and said almost in unison, "You do?"

"Yes, let me speak to him."

"Wait, Davis." Hollie handed the phone to Maddy. "Davis, you still there? Maddy, Angie's friend, wants to talk with you. She has information about the boss. Here she is."

"Sir, I'll be brief. I've been working undercover with Hunter Hines, a man you're familiar with as Angie's stepbrother. He also is a Marine on special assignment. We've been tracking the leader of an eco-terrorist group. This man has been responsible for several bombing threats at military bases."

Davis's voice had taken on a lethal calm. "He planned the attack on Pier 69?"

"Yes, sir. Brandon Billow, but we think that's an alias. He's been working with a guy named Gator."

MEN UNDER FIRE   133

"The guy who Grayce believed tampered with her brakes?"

"Yes, he is the same. I just notified Hunter of the bomb situation. He's been tracking Gator. And sir, Hunter witnessed Dr. Walters getting into a car with someone he suspects might be one of Gator's associates less than ten minutes ago. We don't have an ID on him yet."

Ugly, gross fear shook Nick's body. Dr. Walters had been taken on his watch. His mind reeled with the implications of how he'd failed to protect Dr. Walters from the terrorists she had stumbled upon. Thank God Hunter was protecting her.

"Why in the hell would Hunter allow Grayce to get into the car?"

Nick knew the answer before Davis asked. If the FBI was tracking a suspect, they'd want to glean as much information as they could before intervening.

"Sir, Hunter is following Dr. Walters and has put the FBI on high alert."

"Grayce is a hostage and all he's doing is following?" His anger spilled over, rushing into the harsh way he breathed into the phone.

"Hunter doesn't want to spook the suspect by calling out the cavalry. We don't know if this man is connected to Brandon Billow."

"But you do know that Gator is connected to Brandon Billow, who tried to blow up Pier 69."

"Yes, sir."

"Give me Hunter's number. Which way were they headed? Do you have an ID on the car?"

"You'll have to ask Hunter about the car. I've been pretty busy here, sir."

"Where are they?"

"I-5 south. Sir, Hunter Hines will protect Dr. Walters at all costs."

Nick watched the change in Hollie with the news. Her face went a stark white, her eyes filled with unshed tears, and she chewed on her lower lip. He pulled her closer to his side. Fear and anger made her stiff against him. He understood both feelings since he had them in spades.

Hollie pulled away from him. "We've got to find her. If anything happens to her..." Hollie swallowed hard.

Maddy touched Hollie's arm. "I'm sorry I've gotten all of you involved, but you've got to trust me. Hunter will never let anything happen to Dr. Walters. I know his skills, and she couldn't be better protected."

Nick was grateful for Maddy's efforts to comfort Hollie, but he knew better than to believe one man could stop terrorists. What if there was another bomb?

Hollie shook off Maddy's hand. "I can't stand still and do nothing. I've already done that once today, and I'm not letting anyone hurt the doctor." Hollie got more vehement as she spoke. She widened her stance, her muscles tightened. She was battle ready with no one to fight. Helplessness wasn't easy for anyone but was most difficult for this woman who had been victimized as a child.

Angie, erect with military bearing, her well-defined muscles tensed and coiled, also looked battle ready. "Maddy's right. My step-brother is a top-notch Marine, and I'd always bet my money on Hunter over any sniveling coward. But it sucks to not be able to do anything to help Dr. Walters. She's in this mess because of me. Maddy, tell us how we can help your investigation. Hollie and I both need to intervene right now."

Nick had learned early on from his sisters not to offer his opinion when not asked. That he believed the FBI could protect the doctor wouldn't be shared with these three women. They reminded him of his sisters—strong, ready to take on anyone who threatened someone they loved. He smiled at the comparison, but he didn't think any of them would appreciate the humor.

Maddy ran her hand through her blond curls. He was still having trouble grasping that she wasn't a drugged-out Marine.

"Angie, will you come with me for the interviews of the members of the eco-terrorist group? You won't be able to ask questions, but with your profiling skills, you can help."

Nick felt ready to defend Hollie if Maddy didn't acknowledge Hollie's need for a job.

Maddy was used to commanding and organizing the troops. "Hollie, you need to get back to your office. I'll send over the list of the suspects, and you'll need to go through the records to see if any of them have a connection to Dr. Walters. See if we can pick up any leads."

Hollie took a second to answer, and Nick knew she was fighting the need to do more. Hollie wanted to kick someone's ass. He got the way she coped. She was really afraid and wanted to take control in the most primitive way.

An astute Maddy didn't miss Hollie's hesitation. "Do you have something else you think will help Dr. Walters?"

Hollie hesitated again and then shook her head. "No." One word expressed all of Hollie's frustration and helplessness.

He wanted to take her in his arms and hold her, take away the forlorn set of her shoulders and head.

Maddy's voice was brisk but not unsympathetic. "It's tough not to be in the trenches for Dr. Walters, but none of us have Hunter or the FBI agents' training. If we want to be of help, we each have to do the jobs we're best at."

Nick took Talley's lead from Hollie's hand and laced his fingeres through hers. "Let's head back to the office. You and I can go through the files."

Hollie nodded. "Sure."

Maddy touched Hollie's arm. "Do you know how many innocent people would've died if it weren't for you three? You're going to have to trust me that Hunter will take down whomever has Dr. Walters."

CHAPTER TWENTY-FOUR

Brandon Billow drove a quarter mile on the access road in the isolated industrial area—an eerie landscape of Seattle's maritime past, too far from the main road for Grayce Walters to break away. The wind blew off Elliot Bay, carrying dust from the dirt road across the windshield. Railcars covered with graffiti sat on the seldom-used track. The shipping workers who moved the freight to trucks and trains had finished their work hours before. No one was around.

Railroad tracks protected by a ten-foot cyclone fence topped with barbed wire ran along one side of the access road. Puget Sound bordered the other. Over the high fence and over the

tracks to Harbor Avenue was an unlikely escape route.

Brandon pulled into the parking spot in front of a welcome sign—Certified Wildlife Habitat. Two other cars sat in the far side of the visitors' parking lot—maybe she wasn't alone.

He turned off the ignition, then reached into the glove box, pulling out a large revolver.

Grayce backed against the seat, away from the shiny, lethal weapon.

"Afraid of guns?" His lip curled into a sneer. "I didn't think there was anything you'd be afraid of. Don't worry. I don't have plans to shoot you...yet." He laughed when she flinched. "My military school training comes in handy."

He tucked the gun into the back of his blue jeans, just like she had seen in the movies. "I learned a lot in military school, the same lessons I learned at home. Men use power to bend the

weak to their will. And now the powerful men will bend to me." He checked his cell phone, and his eyes gleamed with a cruel light. "Five minutes before show time."

He got out of the car and walked around to her door. She could kick him in the chest and make a run. But getting shot when trying to scale the ten-foot fence wasn't exactly a viable

option. She was trapped for now.

He opened her door. "We're going to take a little walk up the hill for the view. You're going to witness how much I learned in my military school training. Impressive what I've

engineered."

Grayce scanned the area, searching for other routes of escape. The path was cut into a large hillside with dense trees on both sides and fences beyond to prevent access to the shipyard.

"Don't try anything funny. I won't hesitate to demonstrate my marksmanship. And I'd hate for you to miss the show."

Grayce shuddered. Icy fear ran down her spine, rushing to the backs of her knees and toes.

He gripped her elbow. "We have to hurry. Damn downtown traffic."

Brandon walked next to her, his gun tucked into his blue jeans. To hide his weapon, he wore a lightweight jacket embossed with a smiling penguin. They walked for at least a

quarter of a mile. As they climbed, they caught views of the parking lots filled with trucks and boats on one side and views of the sound on the other.

A teenage couple emerged, coming around the second curve on the path. They walked arm-in-arm, oblivious to everyone else.

Brandon bent toward Grayce and whispered in her ear as if they were also a couple. His hot breath on her skin sent chills of repulsion. "Don't think I won't hesitate to hurt anyone who tries to stop me and my plan."

Grayce stared at the couple. Little chance that they'd notice her dilated pupils, her swift breathing, or her sweaty palms.

Unaware of Grayce's distress, the couple disappeared around the next bend.

As Grayce and Brandon ascended higher, they had a panoramic view of Puget Sound. Jack Block Park was a peninsula that jutted into the sound with a clear view of the Seattle skyline, the surrounding islands, Vigor Shipyards, and the container terminals.

"Do you see the seals?" He pointed among the barges.

Hordes of seals were lying next to and on top of each other on a floating buoy. More black heads bobbed in the water. Their high-pitched barks carried over the water.

"What do you think will happen to those seals with an oil spill?"

Grayce was horrified. An oil spill in Puget Sound? What was he planning?

"Do you think they care about the seals, the dolphins, all the marine life in Puget Sound? All they care about is the money."

How could she answer a deadly fantasy?

They kept climbing. Grayce was a bit short of breath from Brandon's rapid pace and the sharp incline. Brandon wasn't the least bit winded, which didn't bode well for any attempt to

outrun him. Brandon was in good shape, irrational, and armed. Her only chance against him was her aikido. She had to wait for the perfect moment to use her less-than-hundred-pound weight

against his two hundred pounds and his revolver.

Did Davis realize yet that she was missing? He had no leads to her disappearance, but she had total faith in his skills. It didn't look like he'd be in time for a rescue. She had to act soon.

Brandon pointed to an orange platform thirty feet off the ground eight hundred yards ahead. "Our viewing room." They began the walk up a winding path to the platform.

Brandon turned in a full circle when they arrived at the platform. "The view is perfect. I'd first thought I'd watch from a boat, but this angle is better. More dramatic with Mt. Baker as a

backdrop." His body was coiled in expectation, his face twisted in excitement.

He had brought her here to witness a heinous atrocity. She still wasn't sure what the terrible deed might be.

Brandon checked his watch. "Three minutes. You're going to be mesmerized. I've seen videos of what the explosion will look like, but I keep visualizing it rather like a grand Hiroshima without the nuclear fallout."

"What do you hope to gain?"

"Exposing the authorities who've failed us. Do you know how many oil tankers and oil trains are coming into Seattle? Do you? Do you think the port commissioners care? They're in bed with the oil companies, stuffing their political campaigns with oil money."

"This is all about the oil tankers?"

"I'm sending a message to the men who treat people like they're nothing—not worth their time because they don't measure up."

"Why Pier 69?"

"Nothing gets past you—just like my mother. Very smart, Dr. Walters. Tonight is the port commissioners' meeting."

"Why them? Why not target the oil companies?"

"They argue that they're bringing revenue into the city...they're bringing revenue into their pockets. And what's going to happen when Puget Sound is covered in an oil slick? Or

one of those oil trains explodes near Golden Gardens? Will people care about the revenue?"

Her stomach twisted with his quixotic vision. Was he right?

"Look past the Ferris wheel. Those tourists are never going to forget their ride. It's going to be better than the Fourth of July over

Elliott Bay. And like the celebration of our independence, this is another strike against the men who believe they can walk over the entire world. A few men controlling everyone's destiny. This will show them."

She shivered violently, abruptly cold with dread, nauseated from the inhumanity. How could she get away from his isolated spot and stop his malicious plan? "You're killing innocent
people."

"It's the cost of doing business. See if the corporate devils like the cost when it involves them."

She kept hoping to wake up and be freed from this grisly nightmare.

"And we have front row seats."

"You'll never get away with it."

"My mother always had to point out the flaws in my thinking. Why my plans were unrealistic. Won't you both be surprised?"

He looked at his watch again. "One minute to D-day—been planning this for years."

Grayce was paralyzed. She couldn't jump off the thirty-foot platform. She couldn't disarm him unless he rushed her.

He walked her to the west side of the promenade. "Look down there. There's Gator and Mitzi waiting for us. I'll be taking a little boat trip—Vancouver Island, and then to Jakarta."

A large powerboat was moored at the dock below them.

Mitzi was tied in the backseat.

He hadn't included Mitzi or her in his plans.

CHAPTER TWENTY-FIVE

Hollie clambered up Broad Street with Nick and Talley. She felt like a walking zombie, unable to feel or process. It wasn't the sharp incline of the street making her short of breath. It was the heavy pressure of paralyzing fear crushing her chest, squeezing her lungs and heart.

Her body recognized and remembered the terror. The memory of the day when she'd proved to be a coward. Cowering in the closet when her father came to her grandmother's house to "get what belonged to him." Her frail grandma had defended her, screaming "over my dead body" while she'd remained hidden in the closet, too afraid to come to her grandma's aid.

Nick squeezed her hand. She knew a concerned Nick watched her, wanting to comfort her, but there was no comfort. Her life was tilting out of control. If only she hadn't left the office, the shameful memories wouldn't have her by the throat, her body wrenching in disgust.

It was her fault the boss was missing. She had been caught up in the chase of the gamers and, if she were really honest, caught up in spending time with Nick Welby—like some teenage twat. And now Dr. Walters, the first person to believe in her since her grandmother, had been taken and possibly injured. Her entire body shuddered in self-loathing.

Always attuned to her moods, Nick stopped and ran his hand along her arm. She had chills in the heat of the summer day. "Can you tell me?"

She didn't want his look of sympathy and concern. The boss could be injured or worse. She shuddered again. She wouldn't, couldn't think.

Nick stopped in the middle of the sidewalk. "Dr. Walters is going to be okay. You've got to believe. Davis is a very competent man, and he isn't going to allow anything to happen to her. And this Hunter guy is right behind her, with the FBI."

Hollie wanted to scream. Words weren't going to take away the panic. "Don't try to sell me a crock of bullshit. You don't know if she's going to be all right. I'm not some Pollyanna. I know how cruel the world is, but the boss is innocent." She dragged her hand away, but Nick again wasn't letting go.

He jerked her hand. "Look at me." Nick sounded furious.

She glanced up to see two spots of color on his cheekbones, his eyebrows flattened, and a white line around his mouth.

"I'm not selling you anything. And I'm pissed that you think I'd lie to you. I know how much the doctor means to you."

Wow. Nick never got mad at her. Not what she was expecting from the calm and collected military man.

She shifted her weight. Although Nick was pissed, he didn't scare her. Another difference between Nick and other men. "I didn't mean you were lying. I meant that no one knows what will happen."

"I know exactly what you meant. And I know you're worried, and you're blaming yourself, aren't you?"

She looked down at the crack in the sidewalk.

"Hollie, answer me."

"Well, aren't you all bossy? I don't have to answer you or do whatever you want when you're in this pissy mood."

"I'm not bossy. And I don't get pissy."

She could tell he didn't like the portrayal. Must have sounded too girly to him. "You are being bossy and pissy. Look at me. Answer me."

"I'm frustrated and more than pissy because I want to know what's going on in that pretty little head of yours."

She would never tell him. Why did he keep pushing her, wanting to know her dark secrets? She wanted to hit him, pummel him to the ground, make him wince in pain. "Not going to happen."

"You're blaming yourself that you came to the waterfront with me. But there's more—something that happened in the past?'

She resented when Nick understood her, especially when she didn't understand herself. She might have to roshambo him. Then he'd back off.

"And hurting me won't help the bad memories or Dr. Walters."

"No, but it would make me feel better."

He had the nerve to chuckle.

The only way she could kick Nick's ass was by surprising him since he outweighed and outmuscled her. And by the way he scrutinized her, she'd never get the drop on him. "How do you know I have bad memories?"

"Honey, I'm trained to read people, to notice the little differences. Many people's lives have depended on me evaluating people, analyzing their behavior." Nick brushed his hand through his blond hair, an unfamiliar nervous gesture. "But with you, it's different. I don't just read you. It's the damnedest thing, but I can feel when you're suffering."

He didn't try to touch her, which was a smart thing because she didn't want to be touched. "Come on, honey. Talk to me."

"I was remembering something...like you said." Hollie rubbed her sandal back and forth on the crack. She didn't want to look at Nick and see his pity. "My father came to my grandmother's house to take me home...you know why." The fear was creeping back into her. She couldn't keep the disgusting shame at bay. "I hid in the closet, too afraid of what my father had planned for me. And when Grandma defended me, he backhanded my little, frail grandma. I stayed hidden, too afraid to come out. It was my fault my grandma got hurt. And today is my fault. If I hadn't gotten caught up in hunting the gamers and wanting to be part of an adventure with you, I'd have been in the office."

He tucked a curl of her hair behind her ear. She caught a glimpse of his eyes before she toed the sidewalk. She didn't see any disgust in Nick's face, only love.

"Oh, honey. I'm so glad you had your grandma to defend you. It's the job of adults to protect the young. And I'm betting your grandma didn't regret for a second what she did. Did she?"

She hadn't thought that her grandma was doing what normal parents would do. Her grandma had gone to the lawyer the next day to get formal custody. She'd sworn to Hollie she'd never let her father touch her.

"No, she didn't." Hollie didn't mention that she'd run away from her grandma's house when the custody battle had gone on. Her only way of protecting her grandma since she knew the violence her father was capable of.

"Thank God you had her. Is she still alive?"

"No, she died of a stroke a while back." Hollie had always believed it was the stress of her daughter's and son-in-law's meth addiction that had caused her grandma to die.

"I'm sorry to have never met her or thanked her for protecting you."

Hollie glanced up at Nick. He was smiling at her. He was the strangest and sweetest man she had ever encountered.

"My grandma would've liked you."

The tenderness in Nick's eyes made her want to cry. "I'm glad. Your grandma never blamed you for not protecting her. If you're anything like her, she'd be mad as a hornet and want her grand-daughter spared from protecting her. Am I right?"

Hollie had never considered Nick's take on the ghastly memory. Her grandmother was one tough woman.

"If you had come out, how would your grandmother have stopped your dad?"

The shards of shame embedded in her soul didn't feel as agonizing when shared with Nick. From her teenage viewpoint, she'd always believed it was all her fault. But Nick helped her believe she wasn't a terrible person because her parents didn't love or protect her.

"My parents weren't always as bad, until they started doing meth. Then my world fell apart."

"But you put it back together, and you didn't become like them. And today, because of you, hundreds of people didn't die—innocent people and children visiting the waterfront, going on the Victoria Clipper, riding the Ferris wheel are home safe. Families weren't deci-mated by the act of a coward."

Nick thought she had saved people. "What a crock of..." Hollie glimpsed up at Nick. His blue eyes snagged her in his loving gaze. She shook her head. "I didn't save those people. You and Talley did. You were the brave one who chased a woman with a bomb."

He kept his eyes locked on hers, not releasing her from his warm look. "Talley and I played a part in today's rescue, but if you hadn't pursued the research, the reverse Google search, searched Earthbro's account, we wouldn't have been at Pier 69. Talley and I were there because of you."

Tears burned in the backs of her eyes. She wasn't going to turn into one of those blubbering women who cried over everything.

Nick tipped her chin with his knuckles. "Honey, like you weren't to blame for your father's depraved behavior, you're aren't to blame for Dr. Walters's abduction."

"But I can't let anything happen to the boss. She's my family." The tears started, dripping down her face. "She found me in Teen Feed and offered me a job. She pays me so well that I've got my own place. I have benefits, a cell phone. She pretends that I need the phone in case she needs to contact me. I've become part of Davis's family. I babysit for his sisters. And his Aunt Aideen hired me for a new project. And James. Oh, my God. I've got to call James, and what about the boss's family and Aunt Aideen?"

She couldn't breathe. What would she tell James and Aunt Aideen?

Nick wrapped his arms around her. "Take a breath."

She took a slow breath, but a sob got caught in her throat. And she couldn't stop the other deep sobs hidden in her soul. Secure in Nick's arms, she cried. She cried for the sweet, innocent girl she had been; she cried for her grandmother who would've been happy to know she'd met a man like Nick. She felt a bit of her anger and shame get unhinged, shaken loose.

Nick didn't speak but held her tight, his arms wrapped around her, securing and making her safe, vanquishing all her demons.

Slowly the sobs and tears stopped. She sniffed.

Nick whispered in her ear, his breath hot against her neck. "You need a Kleenex?"

He released her to dig into his pocket. Talley had lain down while she'd cried.

She gave a teary, clogged giggle. "Talley must be confused that we seem to have our weirdest moments in the middle of sidewalks."

"Talley is happy to be wherever you and I are. She has no problem adapting. Come on, girl." He pulled on her lead. "We need to get some lunch."

Talley's ears went up with the word *lunch*.

And Hollie wanted to kiss Nick for not making a big deal out of her meltdown.

"I need to call James right away."

"You can call James in the truck. Or I can call him if you want. And he can call Dr. Walters's family."

Nick grasped her elbow and pulled her to his side.

Having him close eased her runaway heart and the pressure in her chest. "Okay."

"That's my girl. And then we're stopping to get some lunch."

"I couldn't eat at a time like this."

"We'll get carryout. I'm starving and you will eat."

"Bossy much?"

CHAPTER TWENTY-SIX

Nick opened the truck door and placed his hand on Hollie's arm to assist her to climb up the fender. Instead of maintaining his usual restraint he always showed around Hollie, he turned her and wrapped her in his arms, bringing her hard against his body. He was an agitated mess of feelings. What she had survived as a child rivaled the stress of his tours in Afghanistan—easier for him as an adult making choices than for a child victimized by immoral bastards.

He touched his mouth to hers—warm, barely touching. Gathering her closer until her breasts pressed against the solid muscles of his body. He moved his mouth over hers, parting her lips, angling his head to match hers. He poured his turbulent emotions and the depth of his feelings into this one kiss. He tenderly ran his tongue along the seam of her lips, nipping her lower lip, promising with his lips and heart to always cherish her with gentleness and restraint.

He felt Hollie's thundering heart against his chest. She leaned into him and placed her hands on each side of his face, holding him in place. She nipped his lower lip before she swept her little, sweet tongue into his mouth, melding them together. Emboldened, she thrust her tongue in a rhythm that made heat burn through him like a blazing furnace. When she sucked on his tongue, he lifted her against his erection, grinding her against the truck. "Oh, my God," he groaned. "What are we doing?"

He felt her smile against his lips. He smiled back. He was in the middle of the street, after defusing a bomb threat; the doctor had been abducted, and he was smiling. He had wanted her badly for so long. Now she finally wanted him. They'd get through all of the hurdles because they had each other.

He loosened his hold and trailed kisses on the side of her face, her forehead, and her pert, little nose. He rubbed his thumb along her swollen lips. "Honey, that was some kiss."

Her face was filled with a lightness he'd never seen. Her dark eyes were brighter. "I'd say the same about yours."

He lifted her against his chest and placed her in the front seat. "Making out with you makes me hungry. Let's grab lunch and head back to the office."

Talley, who had been leaning out the window during their PDA, yelped when she heard the enthusiasm in Nick's voice.

Hollie turned and patted Talley, who now had wedged her head between the front seats. "You hungry, girl?"

He hadn't planned on the passionate interlude, but it seemed to have helped Hollie to get past her guilt and helplessness. He didn't believe for a minute that she had put her worries about the doctor behind her, but she wasn't cowering any longer.

He reached over and grabbed her hand. "You want me to call James, or are you up for it?"

She shook her head. "No, I've got to make the call."

He felt her tension ratchet up as she dialed James. He kept his focus ahead but felt every shift in her seat and every catch in her breath as she debriefed the doctor's friend. He heard the hesitation in her voice and knew she was trying hard not to cry.

"Okay, James, okay." Now she sounded exasperated.

He was surprised when she handed him the phone. "James wants to talk with you. He wants us to come to the boss's house."

"This is Nick," he said as he held the phone to his ear.

"Nick, you're on a fool's errand." James definitely didn't do diplomacy. "There are no criminals in Grayce's patient load. She and Hollie both would know if there were. Hollie shouldn't be alone in the office at this time."

"She won't be alone." Nick bristled with the idea that James didn't consider him company.

"She needs family right now. And we're her family. I'm hanging up to call Grayce's parents. This is going to be rough, but I know they'll be comforted to have Hollie and Aunt Aideen with them."

"I'll discuss it with her, but it's her call," Nick said.

"Man up, Nick. Don't let her convince you otherwise."

And the guy hung up.

Nick handed the phone back to her. "He hung up on me."

"Yeah, he was pretty upset, but he immediately went into orchestrating everyone. He told me that the boss's parents would be comforted having me close by." She gave a little sob. "He told me I needed to be with my family."

Tears dripped down her cheeks. He took her hand. "I think he's right. But do you think there would be anything to help us in the records?"

She shook her head. "After the boss's brakes were messed with, Davis asked me to do the same thing as Maddy. There's nothing. She's an animal acupuncturist, not a spy."

"If you already knew, why did you agree with Maddy?"

"She didn't want to exclude me. I got it, but I'm not a trained Marine or anything, so I went with the flow to allow her to do her job."

He squeezed her hand. "You know you're pretty amazing, right?"

Color moved up her chest into her neck. She crossed her legs, then shook her head. "No, the amazing ones are you, Angie, Maddy, and Talley—serving to protect our country. I'm sorry I brought you into this, Nick."

The woman couldn't accept compliments. He was going to make his life focus that this incredible woman would know how special she was.

He rubbed his thumb along the inside of her palm. "I'm not sorry to be involved. But I am hungry. We're going to get food."

"I'm still not hungry."

"But I am. And we'll do the drive-through at Dick's and eat in the car on our way to Dr. Walters's house. Okay?"

He had learned over the years that in crisis, basic needs had to be kept up. Food and water were needed despite people's protests. Hollie didn't know she was hungry, but once she had food in front of her, she'd eat. She had already been through an incredibly stressful day. She needed her strength to face what was coming next with the abduction.

Nick watched Hollie sip the chocolate shake. She had devoured her Dick's special burger with mayo and pickle relish and now was working her way through the French fries and shake.

He and Talley always ordered the deluxe—two patties with cheese and mayo. Talley, poor dog, only got the patties, missing the mayo and special pickle relish. Asleep in the back seat, Talley didn't seem bothered by her lack of condiments, French Fries, or milkshake.

Nick had discovered Dick's, a sixty-year-old icon, when he was a starving college student at UW. Dick's built its success on serving a limited all-American menu. Good quality for a cheap price made it a success and a staple for every male in the urban area.

Hollie held a French fry in her hand, about to bite down. He leaned over and took a mouthful of the fry. She pulled her hand back. "Hey, that was mine."

"I'm still hungry," he growled as he angled his head to kiss her lips. He licked the salt from the fries off her lips and then thrust his tongue into her mouth. "Mmm. You taste like a chocolate shake."

Hollie's lips curled into a small smile. "You were right. I needed to eat. And a little time before facing the boss's parents after the whole bomb thing. But we should get going."

"We'll probably get to Dr. Walters's house before her parents do. It's only been fifteen minutes max since we talked with James."

She stopped eating from the greasy fry container on her lap. She stared out the window. "I'm not sure what I'm going to say to them. Their oldest daughter was killed in a car accident. And if anything has happened, I don't think..."

He backed his truck out of the parking spot and headed down Wallingford Avenue. "You don't have to say anything. Being there is the important part."

Hollie faced the window. She had withdrawn. The brief interlude was finished, and harsh reality had crept back. He couldn't mouth platitudes. She'd hate that.

He placed his hand on her thigh. "We'll face whatever's coming together. I'm here and I'm not going anyplace."

She nodded but kept her gaze outside. In a hushed voice, she said, "Thanks, Nick."

They drove in silence, a breeze hardly blowing through the open windows. The smell of fries and burger wrappers intensified in the heated truck.

They both startled when her phone rang. Hollie grabbed the phone out of the cup holder and stared at the screen. "It's Davis."

She hesitated to answer. He understood her vacillation. Facing the unknown was sometimes easier than facing reality.

The phone's ring heightened the tension as she watched the screen. She pulled her shoulders back and stuck out her chin, steeling herself to face the news. She pressed the button for speaker. "Davis, any news?"

"She's safe. We nailed the bastard. He's in FBI custody."

Hollie's hands started to shake, and her chest heaved as *she* tried not to cry. "Thank God" was all she could get out.

Nick watched Hollie struggle to swallow. Her lips quivered. "Is she okay?"

Nick rubbed her thigh, trying to soothe her.

"Yes. She's doing better than I am." Davis's self-deprecating laugh echoed in the truck's cab. "Honestly, she's going to be the death of me. I never want to go through this again. Hollie, she wants you to call her parents and James right away. She's being questioned by the FBI. We'll be awhile."

"Will do, Davis."

CHAPTER TWENTY-SEVEN

Hollie searched for the boss's car when she and Nick pulled in front of the turn-of-the-century craftsman's bungalow. Neither the boss's beat-up Subaru or Davis's black Beamer was visible. The FBI must still be questioning the boss.

Sunflowers blossomed around the front porch. The boss was partial to sunflowers and homegrown vegetables. Hollie spotted the small garden with the lopsided scarecrow they'd made together from rejected clothes retrieved from Teen Feed's donation bin. Hollie rubbed at her eyes, fighting back tears. The boss was safe. This was the moment of celebration.

Nick came around the truck and opened the door. He lifted her out of the truck. "This has been one of hell of a day! You ready?"

"Yeah. But pretty crazy, right?"

Nick held on to her as he opened the back door. Talley jumped out and loped through the yard before heading to James, who had walked out of the house upon their arrival.

From the front porch, James twittered in a dramatic voice, waving a glass in his hand. "All hail! Our hero and heroines have arrived after saving the city of Seattle."

Hollie shook her head. How did James know about the bomb? She hadn't told him. When she had spoken to him, she'd been too upset to explain.

Nick said under his breath, "Oh, shit."

Hollie giggled. She'd never giggled before Nick. She was doing a lot of things she had never done. Tonight she hoped to be doing things with Nick she'd never done with anyone and had never desired until Nick.

"How the hell did he find out?" Nick asked.

When Maddy, Angie, and Hunter Hines joined James on the expansive front porch, Hollie immediately knew the source.

Nick muttered under his breath again. "Double shit. I really don't want to rehash this afternoon, do you?"

Hollie laced her fingers through his large, warm hand. "No, I want to see the boss and then go home with you."

Nick stopped in his tracks, then pulled on her hand, bringing her next to him. "What are you saying, Hollie?"

She closed the inches between them, rubbing her chest against his. "You know exactly what I'm saying, Nick Welby. I want you to follow through on all those promising looks and touches."

Hollie loved the way Nick's breath caught and his lips parted for faster breath. "Honey, you're killing me. I've gotta walk into a house full of strangers."

"Man up! You're a hero." She patted his chest, and then she started forward. "Don't worry. We won't stay long."

Nick pulled her back and growled next to her ear, sending sensations surging down her body. "You've got that right. And every time I look at you in there, I'm going to be thinking of what I'm going to do to you, naked in my bed."

She gasped. Her heart beat harder, faster. She shouldn't have started the game. She had only wanted to tell him that tonight was the night, not seduce him. And instead, she was the one seduced. He had turned her into a boneless heap with his husky voice and his erotic words. She wouldn't be able look at him.

James had come down the steps and swooped her into a big hug. "Oh, my God. Grayce is trying to kill me. The stress I've been through in the last hours, worrying about her."

She giggled. It was classic James to make himself center stage. But she understood it was all an act to protect his sensitive feelings. She had heard the fear in his voice when she'd told him about the abduction.

James held her at arm's length. "What's this? Hollie giggling? Not trying to flip me over or use every four-letter word known to mankind?"

She teased, "I think the boss might have suffered a little bit more than you did."

James turned toward Nick. "You must be a good influence on the runt."

Hollie snorted.

"Oh, there's the girl I know." He swept his arm in a wide gesture toward them. "Come on in, kids. We need to hear about today's adventures."

Hollie reached for Nick's hand when they went up the steps. The boss's parents waited at the top of the steps.

Mrs. Walters was the first to hug Hollie. She was tiny and petite and generous and gentle like her daughter. "We've been so worried. I'm glad James had the idea for us to gather here to wait. Thank God the waiting didn't last long and you're both safe."

Hollie didn't know what to do with her hands, so she patted the small woman on the back. Mrs. Walters held tight and didn't release her until Aunt Aideen came out of the house. "My girl. I'm glad you arrived safe and sound. Now I need to see Grayce, my nephew, and, of course, Mitzi, and all will be right in the world." The big woman wrapped her massive arms around Hollie. "We heard about the bomb at Pier 69. Thank God you and your young man are safe." She looked up at Aunt Aideen's face. There were tears and warm concern in her eyes.

Hollie heard Mrs. Walters sniff, with tears dripping down her cheeks. Mrs. Walters again enfolded Hollie in her arms.

The unknown waiting after their older daughter's tragic death would've been hell for the boss's parents. "I'm sorry. It must have been so hard for you and Mr. Walters."

"Grayce and you both in danger in one day. It's too much for Mike and me. Our precious girls in trouble."

Hollie sucked in a breath and fought back tears. Mrs. Walters considered her one of her girls. She looked around, trying to find a way to escape the confusing feelings, and caught Nick watching her as he introduced himself to Mr. Walters and Hunter Hines. She raised one eyebrow. What was she supposed to do? The poor woman needed comforting.

James appeared on cue. "Moet Chandon." He carried out a tray filled with beautiful, long-stemmed glasses filled with champagne. "Lucky I brought my supplies. Grayce doesn't have a bar." James handed around the filled glasses as he kept his monologue going. "Unless you call one bottle of wine a bar. And no flute glasses. Who can live without flutes? I definitely know what I'm getting her and Davis for a wedding present."

James brought the group to total silence with his mention of a wedding.

Mrs. Walters said in a stern voice, "James Weston, do you know something that Grayce's parents don't know?"

James laughed. "Of course not, Christine. But if you had seen them fighting after Grayce's accident, you would know they're meant for each other."

Hollie's eyes collided with Nick's, who was studying her face. His vivid blue eyes captured and wouldn't release her from his intense, demanding gaze. She couldn't look away.

Aunt Aideen, holding a glass of pale gold, raised her glass. "To Grayce and Davis!"

Everyone raised their glasses, cheered, then drank to the toast. It was Hollie's first sip of champagne. The bubbles tickled her nose, but the taste was smooth and not too sweet and went down easily. All was good in the world.

And then James ruined it by raising his glass again. "And to our other lovebirds. To Nick and Hollie."

She felt heat moving through her entire body, and she knew her face was turning a blotchy red. She didn't know what to do or say. She couldn't disagree, but she hadn't been ready to publicly announce her relationship.

Nick moved toward her, put his arm around her, and clinked her glass. He then raised his glass. "To Hollie." And then he smiled down at her, his full-wattage smile with crinkles, and she was a goner.

She looked up to find everyone smiling at her, sharing in her happiness. She smiled back. She'd remember this moment her entire life. All she needed was for the boss to arrive to make tonight perfect.

And as if the evening weren't weird and wonderful enough, Davis drove up.

Grayce, with Mitzi following, came bounding out of the car and into her mother's arms.

Both women started to weep while whispering to each other.

James, after wiping the tears away with a polka dot handkerchief, said, "There's another bottle in the house and food. Please come inside."

Nick kept his arm around her as they walked into the house. Maddy, with Hunter Hines standing behind, waited for them in the center of the boss's small but comfy living room. Hollie didn't need small talk about bombs or abductions. She wanted to apologize to the boss and leave with Nick. And although Nick tried to make her feel better, she still knew she'd let the boss down.

Maddy touched Hollie's arm. "I want to apologize if I was abrupt with you down on the waterfront. I had been undercover for eight weeks with Brandon, and I didn't read the signs that he was our suspect. I was fooled by him. He kept hitting on me and..."

Of course he was hitting on her. Hollie hadn't noticed until now how attractive Maddy, with bouncy blond curls and big blue eyes, actually was. When she'd met the Marine on the waterfront, her mind had still been reeling that Maddy wasn't a drug addict. She looked like Nick's kind of woman.

Hollie glanced up at Nick, who was staring down at her. The hungry way he looked at her said he was thinking of his promise. Warmth slid down her throat, to her breasts, her stomach and lower. Nick wanted her—a Goth, dark-haired, not petite by any standards, and definitely not a blond, bouncy chick.

Maddy looked between her and Nick. "You both did an incredible job."

Hunter Hines stood close to Maddy. His dark eyes and dark hair resembled his sister, Angie, who was chatting up James over by the refrigerator, like old friends.

Hunter turned Maddy toward him and, in a decisive voice, said, "You didn't report this to me."

Maddy's relaxed posture changed in the blink of an eye. She wasn't the cute blond but a Marine all over. She stood taller and looked Hunter in the eye. "He was a guy acting like a guy... nothing suspicious about his behavior. I'm not sure now if it was an act or not."

Hunter's strong, square jaw jutted farther out. "You should've told me."

Hollie watched the interplay. This was about more than their operation. She recognized the alpha male's possessive need on Hunter's face, similar to Nick's. Hunter Hines definitely was interested in Maddy, and not as a fellow Marine.

Maddy had to stretch to look Hunter in the eye. "And what would you've done?"

She had learned that Maddy had lived on the streets before she'd joined the Marines. Maddy was probably escaping a horrendous family or possibly an abusive foster care family. But it looked like Maddy was not one who had slipped through the cracks. She hadn't been beaten down. She was good at giving back.

Hollie heard the boss's voice at the door and rushed over. "Boss, it's my fault. Nick and I should've stayed at the office."

The boss, like her mom, wrapped her arms around Hollie and held her tight. "Nothing was your fault. The only person at fault is Brandon Billow." The boss had never hugged her before. Hollie, probably because of the champagne and the stress, hugged her back.

Nick followed Hollie to the doorway. He waited until the women released each other. He pulled Hollie to his side. "I'm sorry, Dr. Walters, but I don't think we could've made a difference if we had stayed at the office. Brandon Billow followed you to Mrs. Leary's. When Hollie and I found the chat about the group meeting at Pier 69, we had to act."

"You three stopped a bomb from exploding. The FBI agent told me how Talley uncovered the bomb in one of the protestor's backpacks. Obviously, our heroine is tired from her adventures." The boss pointed to Talley and Mitzi crashed on the floor, sleeping side by side in the center of the room.

Hollie could see how the exhaustion began to catch up with the boss. Her hand wobbled when she raised her glass. "I want to make a toast to our heroes and heroines. Everybody raise your glass to thank them for preventing a disaster today."

Then James raised his glass again. "And to the person who started the whole adventure. Without her, Angie wouldn't have been found, the plot to bomb the waterfront wouldn't have been foiled, and Grayce wouldn't have been abducted. Let's raise our glasses to our dear friend Emily Chow."

Everyone said in unison, "*Jaaaaames.*"

And then everyone started to laugh.

Hollie looked around at the full circle of family and friends. It felt right to share this moment with them. It felt right to be part of the group.

Aunt Aideen stepped forward, a glass of Scotch in her hand. "The adventure all began with a prediction."

All eyes turned toward Aunt Aideen.

"I read Grayce's tarot cards. They predicted she would go on a dangerous adventure, and in the end, she and Davis would protect each other and strengthen their relationship. The cards

never lie. I'd like to make another prediction," Aunt Aideen said.

Davis and Grayce shouted simultaneously, "No!"

The large woman gave a belly laugh. She raised her glass of Scotch. "All I was going to say is *A h-uile là sona dhuibh's gun là idir dona dhuib*, which means 'long life will come to all in the room.'"

CHAPTER TWENTY-EIGHT

Nick took Hollie's hand and led her outside to the small cedar deck of his rental house on the north shore of Lake Washington.

"I've got a great view of the meteor showers. Maybe later we can watch them from my sleeping bag."

She walked to the edge of the deck and looked up into the black, velvet sky.

In August in the Northwest, meteor showers could be seen in the night skies. Hollie remembered childhood summer nights with her friends in an open field watching the streaks of light, dust particles from a comet, lighting up the night skies—a magical moment preserved from her childhood and now recreated with Nick. She didn't believe in fairy tales, but all the forces of nature had brought her together with this man at this moment, enough to make her believe.

Nick came up behind her, wrapped his arms around her waist. She leaned back into his hard muscles, his strength. She could feel his warm breath on her neck, his erection pressing against her.

She had been nervous on the drive over, worrying about her

ability to allow tonight to happen, but Nick seemed to understand. He hadn't said anything, he just held her hand. He was quite an amazing man. And she knew if she had said she wanted to go home, he'd honor her wishes.

She turned in his arms to face him and wrapped her arms around his neck. "Later, we can look at the meteors." She kissed him like she had been fantasizing about, the way he had kissed her. She didn't go for subtlety. She thrust her tongue into his wet mouth, exploring the moist space, savoring the taste of Nick.

He gasped when she took his tongue into her mouth and sucked. Nick's response—the tightening of his body against her, his hard, fast breathing—excited her. His calloused hands were exploring under her tank top. Light touches to her sides, under her breasts, down her stomach, giving sensual promises with his touch, ramping up her need with each gentle stroke. His tongue followed the beating pulse in her neck. She leaned against him, wanting him.

Breathless, Nick whispered against her neck, "Honey, you okay?"

His touch and his hot breath on her hypersensitive skin made her restless. She was struggling for air and words. "Nick, I'm more than okay. But can we lie down? I don't think I can stand much longer."

Nick swept her into his arms in one easy motion. "I'd love to lie down." Holding her tight against his chest, he lifted her and moved into the house. He carried her as if she weighed nothing, through the small house to a back bedroom. The room had a double bed and one bedside lamp. Nearby on her bed, Talley was out to the world.

Nick's voice was rough and gravelly. "Do you remember my promise of you naked in my bed?"

She gulped around the bubble of excitement rising in her throat. She snuggled closer to his chest and molded against the rigid muscles. "Nick, how could I forget?"

Nick slowly lowered her, sliding his hard body against her, igniting her craving for him. With her breasts pressed against his chest and his erection against her stomach, her body shuddered with need.

Nick stepped back, his hands at his sides. "You know I want you, but I can wait. You've had a horrendous day. You're sure you want to do this? No regrets?"

What she wanted was standing right in front of her, his bright eyes holding hers in a look that stripped away all her defenses. The moonlight glinted in his fair hair and on his skin. She thought he was the most wonderfully beautiful man she had ever known.

She couldn't fight her heart. "I want you... Tonight... Now." And she stepped closer to him, went on tiptoe, and looped her arms around his neck. She felt the sudden jump of his heartbeat against hers, his body tighten, and then his mouth was on hers, his lips filling her with his scent and flavor.

When the kiss ended, they both were trembling. They stared at each other, shocked by the force of their passion.

Nick fisted his fingers in her hair and brought her back against him, devouring her mouth, exploring with his tongue. The calm soldier breathing roughly and out of control was not in the least bit intimidating, only enthralling. She felt no fear. Her father had taught her to fear the brute strength of men, but not for one moment did she confuse Nick's strength and honor with those previous experiences.

He groaned against her neck. "We've got to slow down."

She reveled in the way she made his control falter. "I don't want you to slow down. I've been waiting a long time for you, Nick Welby." She ran her hands over his chest and to his waist. His breaths rasped in and out of his lungs.

Like a man possessed, his mouth was on her—ravenous, demanding. His hands glided over her, lifting her tank top over her head. He stared at her breasts. His look of desperate hunger sent a thrill down her body.

With his open, wet mouth, he kissed his way along her upper body, along her collarbone, but avoiding her breasts. She threw her head back, offering him her sensitive throat and her swelling breasts. He growled as he took little love bites and then soothed them with his abrasive tongue.

She anchored herself by holding on to his strong forearms. Her entire body squirmed in the carnal onslaught.

He released the snap in the front of her bra, freeing her breasts into his hands. "You're so beautiful and..." He lifted one to his mouth, his tongue teasing her nipple until it puckered. "Oh, my God. I've needed to do this for so long."

His words and the sensations shooting through her body made her mindless and boneless. "Nick, I can't stand."

"Okay, honey. Let's get you out of that skirt."

He knelt before her, his hands running down her thighs, putting his face right next to her. She felt embarrassed and excited.

He slowly slid her skirt down her thighs until she stood in only her black thong. "This little lacy thong is what you've been hiding under here all day." His voice was heated and winded. "If I'd known what temptation you hid under this skirt..."

He separated her thighs with his large hands, put his face to her mound, and inhaled. "Your musky scent makes me want to taste you."

She gasped, unable to get air into her lungs.

"Honey, I promise you're going to like it." He kissed a path along each of her inner thighs, sucking on the skin, moving higher. She leaned against the bed, since she didn't know how much longer she could stand with the nervous anticipation thrumming through her body.

He tongued her clitoris through the lace. She started to tremble, her legs weakening, and she grabbed his head for support.

Nick wrapped an arm around her bottom, supporting her weight, as his tongue was pressed against her. Pleasure soared, and she tipped her head back, arching into the feeling.

He pushed the lace away and started a slow exploration of her clitoris, with his tongue flicking, playing. She moaned and squeezed Nick's hair, trying to hang on when her body was quivering in a rising climax. Nick pushed a finger into her as he pulled on her clitoris and drove her over the edge into a swelling climax. She shrieked in release, her breath and heart thundering.

Nick stood and pulled her against him. His cheeks were red, his breathing harsh. "So sweet. You taste better than I ever imagined. I wanted to spend a lot more time there." He kissed her lightly on the lips. "Maybe later."

She felt weak, her inner muscles throbbed, and she wanted to collapse on the bed. "Nick, I had no idea."

"I know, honey. Let's get you out of the thong." Nick knelt again, and she lifted her trembling legs for him to remove her panties.

He hoisted her up against him as he pulled back the covers, then laid her gently on the bed. "This is exactly how I imagined you in my bed with your hair across my pillow."

She lay nude in his bed and felt no shyness, only anticipation of what would come next with the gorgeous man.

He stood over her, his eyes burning with lust, with his erection pushing against the seam of his jeans. He bent down to smooth her hair away from her face. "I love the way you shriek. I want to make you shriek all night long."

Her heart pounded against her chest as he aroused her again with his deep look and erotic promise. She had to touch him. She wanted him on top of her. "I need you now, Nick."

"Let me get out of these clothes." He peeled out of his jeans and threw off his T-shirt in seconds.

Nick Welby without clothes was an impressive sight with his broad, hairy chest, muscular thighs, and his jutting erection. He reached in the bedside stand.

Heat and liquid pooled between her legs watching a naked Nick Welby roll on a condom.

He looked up and snagged her in his intense look. "Honey, are you afraid?"

That was her Nick. Always thinking of her and her feelings although he was more than obviously wanting her.

"Nick, I'm not afraid. Not after that...what just happened. I know you'll make it good. I trust you."

Nick leaned over and rubbed her lower lip with his thumb. "Well, I'm afraid. I don't want to hurt you."

Hollie stretched out her arms to him. "I'm not believing you're afraid of anything."

He chuckled, then covered her with his weight. The heat of his solid body and his soft chest hair rubbing against her already sensitive nipples agitated and soothed her at the same time. Nick sank his tongue into her mouth as he nudged against her mound. And suddenly she was on edge, restless, wanting more.

"Open your legs for me." Nick spread damp kisses along her neck, making her feverish.

She wrapped her legs around his back, pulling him closer. Nick growled, and he slowly pushed into her partway. He whispered against her mouth. "How does that feel?"

How could he be asking her how it felt? She was a bundle of fervor. "Good, Nick. Good."

He withdrew and pushed in again. She felt the pressure of stretching, being invaded.

He rumbled near her ear, "Honey, you're so tight." Then he took her mouth, plunging his tongue in and out before he moved down and drew her nipple into his mouth.

He pressed farther into her as he sucked harder on her nipple. She moaned and lifted her hips, angling herself to have all of Nick inside her, all of Nick penetrating her. She couldn't breathe, overcome with the need for him to fill her.

He withdrew and thrust into her completely and stopped.

She felt a burning pressure—no pain, just the wondrous satisfaction of Nick filling her, of being united.

Straining, buried inside her, Nick sucked in a deep breath. "I hurt you. I'm sorry."

"Just a little bit. I'm okay. And Nick, can you keep moving?" She grabbed the tight muscles of his backside, urging him to help with the peaking sensations.

He stayed still but captured her mouth. "I'm planning on moving. Moving to make you very happy."

He drove into her hard and fast. "I'm sorry, I can't slow down, but I've waited for you so long." He grabbed her hips and worked a frantic rhythm that was building her need.

The mighty wave rolled over her, emptying her mind of all thought, filling her with pleasure and joy. He lowered his head to her neck, his frenzied breathing matching his thrusts. And as she cried out in ecstasy, he bellowed and gave in to his own powerful release.

He collapsed on top of her. His rapid breathing, his weight pressing her into the mattress, and the gentle way he kissed her lips were bliss. She hugged Nick close, not wanting him to move. Who would've thought she'd ever want a man's body over her? Miracles did happen.

Nick rolled off of her and propped his head on one elbow, searching her face. His face was relaxed and replete. "Honey, I knew we were going to be good together, but that just went beyond any fantasy I had about you."

"Me too, Nick. Beyond anything I imagined." She sighed, more than overwhelmed with all the emotions bombarding her.

He kissed her, barely touching her lips, a soft brush. "Was it terribly painful?"

She rolled to her side to face him and touched his bristly jaw and then traced his full lower lip with her finger before taking a love nip. "Hardly at all. You made it all wonderful."

"Thank you for..." He stuttered, "You don't know what means to me to be the first and last man to make love with you."

Confused, she asked, "Last?"

He growled and rolled her on her back and bent over her, his weight on his arms. "I love you, Hollie. And I want to be with you and you with me—no one else."

Unable to squeeze out a single word, she shook her head.

"No? You don't want to be with me?" His voice got quiet.

"No, we can't love each other, we just met."

Nick studied her face, watching her intently. "You just said 'we' can't love each other. Are you saying you love me?"

"Oh, Nick. I don't know much about love, but I'm willing to learn when it comes to loving you."

"It's all a man needs to hear. I love you, Hollie. And I promise to cherish you as you deserve." He took her lips in tender possession. "And if you're willing to learn, I've got a few more lessons for tonight."

Hollie smiled back at his full-wattage smile that had captured her from the first moment she'd met him. "Nick, that's all a woman wants to hear."

A NOTE TO MY READERS

Dear reader,

Thank you for reading *Men Under Fire!* I hope you enjoyed it. If you did, please help others find it by writing a review!

Reviews mean so much to an independent author and I love reading them!

And if you sign up for my newsletter to see the latest news, and join my readers group to be the first to hear about special events, excerpts, and unseen previews!

Visit my website: http://www.jackidelecki.com to read more about the adventures of Grayce Walters, animal acupuncturist in *An Inner Fire.*

MARRIAGE UNDER FIRE: BOOK FOUR

Maddy Jeffers always chose daring over caution.

With her pelvis thrust forward, she countered her absurd posture by throwing back her shoulders. Since she was on the carpet, she might as well make it a Hollywood red carpet. In her three-inch knockoff designer heels, she placed each foot very firmly and carefully to avoid teetering down the silent, sterile hallway of Seattle's Henry Jackson Federal Building. The gunmetal-gray walls and the Pine Sol smell of a moldering, uncaring bureaucracy took her right back to her years as a foster child—in another government building, her future in question again.

Instructed to report out of uniform, she had been in a major quandary. Should she arrive dressed as the ecoterrorist she'd been during her last undercover assignment to make it easier for them to reprimand her? Or should she look like any other office worker?

Hunter Hines, her partner on the assignment, had texted her to report at 2000 to JFB.

The man could have given her a heads-up about what she faced; Marines took care of their own. Of course, Hunter wouldn't allow anything like human emotions or the dangers of that particular assignment affect his report.

Speak of the devil, there was Hunter, waiting in front of the glass door to the FBI office. She surreptitiously dried her sweaty palms on her tight black dress and added swagger to her slow, agonizing walk. No way would she admit, even under the threat of torture, that her killer shoes were killing her.

His dark, piercing eyes took in every step. Did she imagine it, or had his rigid Marine posture stiffened and his dark olive skin flushed when he saw her? Perhaps she wouldn't be the only one to suffer today.

Dressed in a dark suit with an open oxford blue shirt, with his long, inky black hair, he looked the part of a billionaire playboy or techie—the cold devil looked mighty good. She tried to ignore the fact that he was sexy as hell and remember he was a pain in the ass.

"What the—?" His eyes narrowed and she waited to hear the censure in his voice. "You don't look like a Marine."

What was a Marine working undercover supposed to look like? And why was it always an issue for a woman, but never a man? He didn't look like a Marine today, either.

The young saleswoman at Macy's told her this was an office dress. How would Maddy know what women wore to their jobs? She had never worked in an office and hoped to God she never would.

Her chin hitched up an inch. She was immune to his snide, unanswerable remarks. "Good morning, sir. My instructions were to report out of uniform." No matter what she wore, she was a Marine, through and through. "I'm blending in."

"Blending in? You call that sexy getup blending in?"

She looked up at him with her best innocent face. "You think it's sexy?"

She pulled at the snug dress riding part way up her thighs.

He watched her movement with his usual eagle-eyed focus. She didn't miss the hitch in his breath and the way his muscular throat rippled when he swallowed. "Think what?"

Hunter Hines lost for words—she was already feeling better.

ABOUT THE AUTHOR

Jacki Delecki is a USA Today bestselling romantic suspense author whose stories are filled with heart-pounding adventure, danger, intrigue, and romance.

Her books have consistently received rave reviews for her three bestselling suspense series: Contemporary romantic suspense *The Impossible Mission Series*, featuring Special Force Operatives; *The Grayce Walters Series*, contemporary romantic suspense following a Seattle animal acupuncturist with a nose for crime; and *The Code Breakers Series*, Regency suspense set against the backdrop of the Napoleonic Wars.

Jacki's stories reflect her lifelong love affair with the arts and history. When not writing, she volunteers for Seattle's Ballet and Opera Companies, and leads children's tours of Pike Street Market.

To learn more about Jacki and her books and to be the first to hear about giveaways, join her newsletter found on her website.

IF YOU LOVED MEN UNDER FIRE YOU WILL ALSO ENJOY...

Grayce Walters Mystery series

An Inner Fire

Women Under Fire

Men Under Fire

Marriage Under Fire

A Marine's Christmas Wedding

The Grayce Walters Romantic Suspense Series 1-4

The Impossible Mission Romantic series

Mission: Impossible to Resist

Mission: Impossible to Surrender

Mission: Impossible to Love

Mission: Impossible to Forget

Mission Impossible to Wed s

Mission: Impossible to Protect

Mission Impossible to Deny

The Impossible Mission Series Books 1-3

Code breaker Regency series

A Code of Love

A Christmas Code

A Code of the Heart

A Cantata of Love

A Wedding Code

A Code of Honor

A Holiday Code for Love

A Code of Wonder

A May Day Code for Love

A Code of Joy

A Secret Code

The Code Breakers Series Box Set

The Code Breakers Series: Holiday Romances